TRUSTING LOVE

EMMA LEIGH REED

Copyright © 2013 by Emma Leigh Reed
Book design by Jesse Gordon

Warning: The unauthorized reproduction or distribution of this copyrighted work is illegal. Criminal copyright infringement, including infringement without monetary gain, is investigated by the FBI and is punishable by up to 5 (five) years in federal prison and a fine of $250,000.

Names, characters and incidents depicted in this book are products of the author's imagination or are used fictitiously. Any resemblance to actual events, locales, organizations, or persons, living or dead, is entirely coincidental and beyond the intent of the author.

No part of this book may be reproduced or transmitted in any form or by any means, electronic or mechanical, including photocopying, recording, or by any information storage and retrieval system, without permission in writing from the author.

To my daughters, Alexa and Rachel.

My wish is that you know how worthy you are. Worthy to be treated as the beautiful young women you have become. Never accept being treated with anything but respect. I love you both!

CHAPTER ONE

Chloe Wilder shot up in bed. She rubbed her eyes with the back of her hands trying to adjust to the dim moonlight that filtered in through the closed blinds. Her heart raced as she took in the shadows that danced around the room. She swiped her hand across her face to wipe away the tears the nightmare left behind. Wrapping her arms around her knees, she hugged herself tight.

This same nightmare had become recurrent. Her arms wrapped around her waist, she whispered, "I won't let anything happen to you."

She pushed the covers off, jumped out of bed, and crossed to the window. It was dark except for the light of the moon. No street lights were lit. There was no better time than now.

She pulled on an old pair of sweat pants and a baggy sweater. She dragged an old tattered suitcase from the closet and started packing. A sense of urgency came upon her as she shoved in the last shirt and closed the suitcase. She glanced around the room and her eyes stopped on a picture of her parents. They held each other, smiling. It was obviously taken at a happy moment. She picked up the picture and looked closer. Sadness and shame overwhelmed her. Holding it close, Chloe closed her eyes and prayed for forgiveness for the mistakes she had made in her life. Putting the picture in her purse, she picked up the suitcase and slipped through the door into the night.

She threw the old suitcase in the backseat of her beloved Toyota. The vehicle was on its last leg, but somehow it kept running. Chloe prayed it would take her far away from this town, and even further from all the pain. She needed a fresh start for her and her baby she vowed to protect.

She drove with her lights on low, praying no one would see her. Turning onto a back road she blew out a sigh of relief as the road lead her out of town. Time was of the essence. She had a small window of opportunity to put distance between Tony and her. Chloe didn't know what had possessed her to get involved with him. He had been quite a charmer in the beginning. Now thoughts of Tony brought only regret and fear. She shuddered at the thought of what he would do when he found her gone.

The night seemed to get blacker as she drove further out of town. Tension knotted her neck and her arms ached from gripping the steering wheel. Chloe forced out a deep breath and turned the radio to a soft rock station. She allowed herself to relax just a fraction after driving for hours into the night.

Miles passed. The sky turned from black to a gray with a tinge of pink in the horizon. Chloe's eyes grew heavy. She found a rest area facing the ocean and pulled in. Locking her doors, she closed her eyes. *Just a few minutes of sleep, then I will keep moving.*

* * *

The house was quiet when Tony slipped inside. He smirked in the dark. Chloe was so predictable—always in bed before he got home hoping to avoid him. He could see through her, but she was easily influenced and good to have around. He made his way to the kitchen to grab a beer. Twisting off the cap, he slipped into living room and sat down. His legs sprawled in front of him he lounged back in the easy chair.

Chloe had been young when he had found her. She was eager for love and he gave it to her. Well, maybe not the love she had been looking for, but he didn't care what she needed. He did feel sorry when he saw her tears but now he's bored and ready to move on, but can't. She overhead too many conversations and knew too much.

He sighed and placed the empty bottle on the table next to him, stood and started upstairs. Something had to be done with her. He slipped into the bathroom off the bedroom and turned on the light. Tony expected to see Chloe huddled on the edge of the bed. He did a double take when he realized the bed was empty.

What the hell. He flipped on the bedroom light. She had been there. The covers were tossed aside. He pulled open a bureau drawer. Her clothes were gone. His fists clenched at his sides as he raced downstairs.

He pulled his cell phone from his pocket and punched in a number.

"She's gone... I don't know where, just find her and fast..." He disconnected, picked up the empty beer bottle and flung it against the wall. The glass shattered into tiny pieces that sprayed across the hard wood floor. "Chloe, what have you done?"

CHAPTER TWO

A rap on the window startled Chloe and she flew up. A uniformed officer stood smiling at her. She rolled down the window an inch.

"Miss, are you okay?"

"I'm fine. Did I do something wrong?" Chloe's voice trembled.

"Well, this is a no parking zone."

"I-I'm sorry. I didn't realize. I was tired and didn't want to fall asleep driving."

"It's fine. Name's Jayden Peterson. I'm the Chief of Police in this town. If you're hungry or need coffee, there's a great diner down the road. I was headed there myself."

Chloe glanced at her clothes. "I'm not sure. I probably ought to be moving on."

"Let me buy you a cup of coffee for the road. You probably could use a bite to eat, too. Consider it a 'welcome to our town' gesture. Anyone who lives in Arden would do the same. It's small town hospitality." He assured her with a smile.

She hesitated a brief moment, but the rumbling in her stomach couldn't be denied. "Okay, but just a quick bite."

"Great. Follow me. It's just down the street."

Pulling out on the road behind the police car, Chloe's mind was a whirlwind. Why did she accept this invitation? Just where in the world was Arden? Didn't matter; anywhere wasn't far enough from Bridgeport. A glance in the rearview mirror showed a pale, scared face with huge eyes. She groaned and regretted instantly agreeing to go for breakfast. But her unborn child was the most important thing right now and they both needed something to eat.

She parked the beat-up hatchback beside a large truck hoping to hide the pathetically looking excuse she called a car. Sweeping her hair into a ponytail with the elastic band she always kept on her gear shift, Chloe pinched her cheeks to add some color and got out of the car. Jayden was waiting beside his patrol car.

"Glad you decided to grab some coffee at least." Jayden held the door to the diner. "This is the best food in Arden."

"Thanks," Chloe murmured.

"Here. This booth is quiet. Order anything you like." Jayden passed a menu across the table and discreetly walked to the counter to get coffee. The diner was small and she could hear the whispers from the counter.

"Who's the girl, Chief?" Her name tag said Carla. She grinned at the police man like an old girlfriend.

"Something get by you, Carla?" Jayden teased her and it brought a smile to Chloe's face.

"Found her parked at the beach sleeping in her car. She's looking pretty hungry. Tab is mine for whatever she eats."

"You got it." Carla picked up the coffeepot and headed towards the table. "Coffee, sweetie?"

"Yes, please." Chloe glanced up to find a middle-aged woman smiling at her and immediately felt at ease. "What do you recommended?"

"Anything and everything. Best food around, if I do say so myself." Carla slid into the booth across from Chloe. "I'm Carla. I own this diner. You're new to town?"

"Just passing through." Chloe got busy perusing the menu.

"Well, if you decide you want to stay, I can recommend some rooms for rent." Carla stood up. "Even could offer you a job. I could use some help around here."

"I really don't know if I'm staying, but thanks." Chloe handed her the menu. "I'll have the special, though, and a glass of milk."

"You got it." Carla headed for the kitchen.

Chloe poured cream into the coffee then leaned back in the booth. The diner was good size and almost completely full. No one seemed to be paying much attention to her despite her disheveled appearance. She sighed and relaxed a bit.

Her eyes fell upon Jayden sipping his coffee. She smiled shyly. Her stomach tightened in anticipation as he made his way towards the booth.

"May I join you?" He waited for a response.

"Of course. Th-thank you for bringing me here. I really appreciate you overlooking me sleeping in the no parking zone."

"We don't throw people in jail for that kind of stuff around here." He chuckled. "Just enjoy breakfast. It's on me."

"I don't have much money, Office Peterson, but I can afford to pay for my own breakfast." Chloe met his eyes.

"I'm sure you can. But it's already tended to. Consider it a welcoming gift. Arden is a safe place to be." He gestured to Carla for more coffee.

"Really, I can't accept that."

"Okay. But I'll let you take that up with Carla. She expects us to be friendly around here."

Chloe played with her coffee mug. It had been a long time since she relaxed for just a little bit and her instincts were saying Arden was a place she could begin to let down her guard. Would it be safe enough for her to stay a little while?

Carla brought her breakfast and Chloe dug in with gusto. She hadn't realized how hungry she was until the food was placed in front of her. She slowed down and glanced up. Jayden was watching.

"Hungry?" He grinned.

"I guess so." Chloe shrugged. "Might as well fill up now. Not sure where I will be when it's time for my next meal."

"Are you headed somewhere in particular? I'm sorry, I didn't catch your name."

"It's Chloe, Chloe Wilder." Chloe sat back and considered the question. "I'm just looking for a change of pace and something new. Didn't give it much thought really." She looked down at her hands folded in her lap and fought to keep the tears in check. It all seemed so logical last night after the nightmare, but now in the daylight things were not as clear.

"Well, we always have room for one more in Arden. It's a small town and a close knit one. We take care of our own." Jayden picked up his hat. "Thanks for the company. It was nice to meet you, Chloe."

Jayden threw a tip on the table and walked over to Carla. Chloe finished her meal and reached for her purse. Opening her wallet, she blinked hard at the threat of tears flowing as she saw she had only seven dollars in her wallet. Just enough to pay for what she had eaten.

"It's all paid for, honey." Carla slid into the booth. "Don't you worry about it."

Chloe gave her a smile. "Thanks."

"I don't want to overstep, but I really could use some help for at least the next few weeks. The girl who was helping all summer left for college and now I'm left shorthanded. Could you spare a few days to maybe help me out?"

Chloe studied Carla. "I could use the extra money, but have nowhere to stay. And not much money."

"Don't worry about that, I have a huge house and with a vacant in-law apartment. It's yours to use as long as you want. If you stay longer than a few weeks, we'll talk about rent."

"Thank you. I don't know…" Chloe's voiced trembled then trailed off. Why was she always so close to breaking down in tears?

"Let's get you settled in. Is it okay if I have you follow Jayden to the apartment while I finish up this shift?" Carla stood.

"Yes, of course." Chloe rose and smiled again. It felt good to be staying in a quiet place, a safe place. She just needed to find out how far she had made it from home… from Tony.

Carla called for Jayden. They talked quietly, as Chloe stood and walked towards them trying to look sure of herself. Her mind was a spinning as she followed Jayden out of the diner and to her car.

"It's down the road. Not far. Easy walking distance on nice days, if you wanted to."

"I'm sorry?" Chloe looked up and saw Jayden watching her. "I guess my mind was elsewhere. I'm ready when you are."

"Okay. Just down the road." Jayden started to turn towards his car and stopped. "Chloe, are you okay?"

"Yes. I'm fine. Tired…long drive last night." She avoided his eyes and started to her car.

* * *

Jayden turned and went to his car. His instincts told him she was hiding something, yet he felt the overwhelming urge to protect her. She looked so fragile and scared. He sighed. The need to protect her was more than his duty as a police office. In the back of his mind, he knew he needed to stop that line of thinking, yet he couldn't help it. Something about Chloe made him want to fold her in his arms and tell her it was going to be alright, whatever that might be.

CHAPTER THREE

Chloe and Jayden parked in front of Carla's large old Victorian home. The light blue paint peeled away from the wood exterior, but the gardens were in full bloom, testament to the love that had been given to them. She stepped out of her car and was taken back to a happier time where laughter filled the air. She could hear her dad laughing as he pushed her higher and higher on the old tire swing in the backyard and she squealed with delight.

She shook her head to clear the memory, put on a smile, and turned towards Jayden. For the first time she really noticed him. He was fairly tall with brown hair cut short. His dark brown eyes reminded her of rich chocolate that she could just melt into. Chloe's cheeks warmed as her thoughts wandered.

She faced the house. "What a great house."

"Yes. It's been in Carla's family forever. It's her baby."

Chloe instinctively wrapped her arms around herself and sighed. Where was she going to raise her child? She wanted a home filled with laughter for her child and yet she saw no hope of that. Everything was bleak.

She went to the back of the car to grab her tattered suitcase. Before she had it out, Jayden was there reaching for it.

"It's okay. I've got it," Chloe insisted, ashamed of the sad shape it was in.

"Don't be ridiculous, Chloe." Jayden tensed. "My mom taught me to be a gentleman. Please, let me carry it."

Chloe stepped back. "Sorry. I'm just used to doing things myself."

They followed a small walkway around the old house to a staircase that led them to the in-law apartment. Jayden pulled out the key Carla had given him and opened the door. Chloe had never seen such a plush apartment. The carpet was a deep burgundy and thick. It was furnished with an overstuffed couch and recliner. A television stood in the corner. She moved through the living room to a room off to the side. A small dinette sat in the corner of the kitchen. It was small, but functional.

She traced the carved wooden trim with her fingers as she walked down the hall which ended at the two bedrooms. She stopped at the small one and sighed. It would be perfect for the baby—if she stayed that long. She turned and made her way back to the living room, she saw her suitcase by the door, but Jayden was nowhere to be found.

Chloe glanced out the large bay window and found him standing out on the small deck overlooking the backyard.

"Beautiful place." She said from the doorway as she scanned the amazing yard, Jayden move towards her and she felt his gaze as he studied her.

"It is. I'm glad you will be helping Carla. She works too much for someone her age."

Her face heated up as he continued to stare. "I'm glad I could help. I don't know how long I can stay though." She turned to meet his eyes.

"Why? Where are you headed?" Jayden asked.

"I don't know. I just don't know what I'm doing." Chloe's voice wavered. She forced herself to look away and took a few steps to the other railing. She needed space between them because she wanted nothing more than for him to hold her.

Where had that come from?

"I don't want to pry, Chloe, but I can't help but wonder what you are running from."

"What makes you think I'm running? I'm just looking for a change of scenery, some place different. That doesn't mean I'm running." Chloe turned. Blinking back the tears she fought to hide.

"Okay. I'm sorry." He stepped towards the yard "If you need anything, let me know. Carla can let you know where to find me."

She nodded and whispered, "Thank you."

Jayden's eyes met hers and held her gaze as he descended the stairs. "Get some rest, Chloe. You look exhausted."

Her eyes followed him as he walked back to his car. The tears she fought to hold back flowed down her cheeks as Jayden drove out of the driveway. She moved back inside and collapsed into the overstuffed recliner. Within minutes she was sound asleep, and for the first time in a long time, it was a peaceful rest.

* * *

Jayden turned his car towards the station and battled his conscience about whether or not he should run a check on Chloe Wilder. He had the definite feeling she was hiding something. He kept telling himself he was protecting Carla by finding more about Chloe. There was such vulnerability about her. Her blue eyes were full of sadness and fear. There had to be more to it than just looking for a change of scenery. She was running. His gut told him so. The question was from what and how bad was it?

He slammed the door at the station and received a glare from his dispatcher. He grabbed another cup of coffee, deep in thought as he stirred it.

"What's eating you?" Betty asked. She had been the dispatcher for the Arden police office all her adult life. She had worked for Jayden's dad before him."Nothing. Just have some stuff on my mind." Jayden set down the spoon and sipped his coffee.

"Humph. So you say. Don't be slamming doors around here. I know your mother taught you better," Betty grumbled as she turned back to her computer screen.

"Sorry, Betty. Yes, I know better." Jayden smiled and moved to his office, closing the door softly. He chuckled.

She got after him about the door when he was kid and ran in to the office to see his dad.

Sitting behind the desk, Jayden flipped on the computer. He sat back in the chair, sipping his coffee, wondering where to start. The curser blinked at him. With a sigh, he pulled up Google and typed in her name. His finger hovered over the Enter key for a brief second before he clicked it.

Nothing.

The screen revealed no results. She was a nobody as far as Google was concerned, no one with a record or internet history that he could find. He sat back and contemplated his next move. Lots of resources were available, but a smile played across his lips as his mind wandered to consider how he would like to just get to know her. The sad eyes had caught him and underneath the baggy clothes he wondered how thin she really was. She had a gauntness about her, she needed someone to take care of her, someone to cook a decent steak for her.

He stood up suddenly and headed for the door. He stopped with uncertainty. Betty's hands never missed a keystroke.

"Headed out again?"

"Yeah. I'll be back later. You can reach me if you need me." Jayden started for the door again.

"Checking up on that new girl in town?"

Jayden turned and looked at her. "How on earth did you know about her already?"

Betty grinned. "I may be old, but I still know what's going on."

"I have some errands to run. I'll be back." He left in a hurry. If Chloe was running, she wouldn't be able to blend in very well with so many busy-bodies in this town. Jayden couldn't shake the feeling that Chloe needed him to protect her.

CHAPTER FOUR

Chloe awoke to an unfamiliar room. Panic gripped her until she remembered yesterday. And Jayden. He had been so kind. She reached for a lamp. No. She needed to keep her wits about her. Another man was not in the cards right now.

Her stomach grumbled and she realized she needed to take care of the baby. She sat there a moment thinking of how to get groceries. She had seven dollars to her name and didn't start work until tomorrow. Walking to the kitchen, she hoped there were at least crackers in the cupboard.

She stood in the center of the small kitchen and wondered where to start? A tug of guilt went through her as she reached for the first door. It was filled with everyday plates and cereal bowls along with a few mixing bowls. Chloe moved onto the next cupboard and found glasses and coffee mugs. Frustrated, she leaned against the counter and closed her eyes. How did she get into this mess?

The doorbell rang and it sent her heart racing.. No one knew where she was. She had been careful to leave her cell phone off. She hesitantly walked to the door and peeked out the side window to see Jayden standing there holding a bag. She opened the door slowly wondering how smart it was for her to continue to talk to him.

"I brought you some groceries. I thought you might not have had a chance to look around town yet or find a grocery store. Just some basics—milk, eggs, crackers, cereal, and some steaks, salad and potato for dinner tonight." Jayden smiled and waited for Chloe to let him in.

"You didn't have to do that. How much do I owe you?" Chloe stepped aside, hoping he would allow her to pay him after she got her first paycheck.

"Not a thing. Just a friendly gesture." Jayden started for the kitchen. "How do you like your steak?"

"I haven't had a steak in a long time. Medium, I guess." Chloe followed him back into the kitchen and watched Jayden take over, putting the milk and eggs in the refrigerator.

"I hope I'm not overstepping, Chloe. I just thought I could cook you dinner. I've had a long week and a steak dinner sounds good on a Friday night. Thought it might sound good to you, too. Of course, I'm interested in hearing about what brings you to Arden, if you feel comfortable talking about it."

Fear gripped Chloe and she struggled to keep her face neutral. "Dinner is fine, but I would much rather hear all about this town since I'm going to be here for a little while." She reached for the empty bag to fold up. Her hands trembled and she forced them to be still, hoping Jayden had not seen.

"Oh, the stories I could tell you about this town." Jayden laughed. "I grew up here. I'll probably never leave."

Chloe let out a breath. He obviously hadn't noticed her uneasiness, or at least he wasn't mentioning it. "You've lived here all your life?"

"Yeah. My mom and dad grew up in this town, too. It's a great town. Tourist fill it up in the summertime, but in the winter, you just get lost in the quietness."

A smile played on his lips as he reminisced. His love for his hometown was obvious.

"What can I do to help?" Chloe interrupted as the rumble in her stomach signaled her hunger.

Jayden chuckled. "Haven't you eaten since breakfast?"

"No, I guess I fell asleep." Chloe's face heated up.

"I'll get the grill fired up. If you want to wash the potatoes and wrap them in foil, I will get them on the grill and then start preparing the steak. You can make the salad." Jayden slipped out the back door onto the deck where a grill stood at the far side.

Chloe sighed and reached for the baby potatoes. She needed to keep her guard up with him. He was a police officer and if anything, could lead Tony right to her without even trying. Tony had a way of making friends with police and winning them over.

She busied herself getting the potatoes ready and took them out to Jayden. He had fired up the grill and was standing on the deck looking out to the ocean.

"I didn't know you could see the ocean from the backside of the house." Chloe stood next to him. The beauty of it was overwhelming. The sky, pink with sunset, ran into the blue of the ocean. It could have been a picture.

"I didn't want to spoil the surprise. I thought you would have explored by now and found it yourself. It's beautiful. Sunset has always been my favorite." Jayden reached for the potatoes in Chloe's hands and paused as his hands grazed hers. The heat from their touch radiated up Chloe's arms. Her eyes locked with his. Time stood still for a moment as they looked at each other, each lost in their own thoughts.

Chloe broke her gaze first and handed the potatoes to him. She turned back to the sunset and hoped he couldn't hear the beating of her heart.

She listened to Jayden get the potatoes on the grill and closed the cover. She felt his presence as he stood close, yet she kept her eyes glued on the water.

"The colors are amazing," he whispered.

"They are." Her soft answer sounded husky to her and she cleared her throat. "So do your parents still live in town?" She moved away to the table off in the corner and sat in the chair.

"Mom is still here. Dad passed away a few years ago. He used to be the police chief."

"I'm so sorry." Chloe's eyes filled with tears as the loss her own parents flashed before her..

"It's okay. He had been sick for quite a while with cancer. Mom's a trooper though. She took care of him right up until the end. Now she volunteers at the hospital in the children's ward."

"Wow. Sounds like she didn't slow down much after your father passed."

"No, not at all. She thinks she still has a lot to give. She is one remarkable woman." Jayden stood and checked the doneness of the potatoes. "I'm going to get the steaks ready. Enjoy the sunset. I'll be back out in a second."

Chloe watched him walk inside and wondered how she'd get through the evening. She felt so comfortable with him, she just wanted to open up and tell him everything, but in the past she had been too open, too naïve, for her own good. Look where it had got her.

She took in the sunset and let her mind wander to memories of her parents. They had been gone now for nine years and she still missed them terribly. Her heart ached remembering the news of the car accident. They had been killed when a drunk driver ran a red light. Tears glistened on her eyelashes. She blinked furiously to clear her vision before Jayden came back outside.

She stood and leaned over the railing. Chloe knew in her gut that this town could be a very positive place to raise a child. She wished she could hide here forever, but didn't have the courage to stay put anywhere for a long time. She couldn't put down roots and just rely on hope that Tony wouldn't find her. Tony wouldn't let her go without a fight...it was the one thing Chloe was sure of. She sighed and hugged her arms around herself.

"Cold?" Jayden slipped up behind her and placed his jacket around her.

She pulled it close. "Thanks. I'm okay."

"Have you had a chance to talk to Carla yet?"

"No. She said she would stop by later to discuss work. Of course, I slept all afternoon. I should see if she is home yet." Chloe made no effort to move.

"We can walk over there after we eat. Relax for now." Jayden smiled, his eyes searching her face.

Chloe, feeling self-conscious, averted her eyes. She needed to pull herself together and keep her defenses up. She looked up and his gaze pulled her closer.

"I don't know how long I will be staying. At least to make a little money while I help Carla, but I can't stay long." She tried to smile, but the emptiness she felt saying those words out loud hit her. She already was sad at the thought of leaving Arden.

"Let's get those steaks on." Jayden turned toward the grill, his mind whirling with the possibilities of what made Chloe so sad and so afraid.

"I'll prepare the salad." Chloe escaped to the kitchen and looked out the window. Jayden turn his back to the house and gazed at the sunset. She pulled his coat closer and closed her eyes. She inhaled deeply and took in the scent of him. Her heartbeat increased at the smell. She didn't want to lie to him.

Shaking her head, she slipped the jacket off her shoulders and laid it over a dining room chair. She ran a hand over it to smooth it out. Sighing, she turned to the salad. After throwing the it together, Chloe set the table. She had just finished when Jayden walked back in through the door with the steak and potatoes.

"Is eating in here okay?" Chloe fiddled with the silverware next to the plate.

"Absolutely fine. It gets a little chilly on the deck when the sun goes down."

They sat at the table and filled their plates. Chloe ate with enthusiasm realizing just how hungry she was. She looked up to meet Jayden's eyes.

"It's delicious." She grinned.

"I see that." He chuckled as he took a bite.

"Sorry, I didn't mean to be rude."

"You weren't. I just have never seen a female put away food ike you can. Okay…maybe my sister."

"You have a sister?" Chloe's fork paused. She was once again hit with a pang of loneliness.

"Yes. She's a couple of years older and protective as anything of her 'little brother'."

"It must be nice to have a sibling. I'm an only child and used to dream I had a brother, or a sister." Chloe dropped her eyes, wishing she hadn't revealed so much about herself.

"Where are your parents?" Jayden's voice was soft.

"They were killed in a car accident years ago by a drunk driver."

"I'm so sorry, Chloe." Jayden's sympathy, so evident in his voice, was almost the undoing of her. She blinked to hold the tears back.

"Tell me about growing up in Arden." She changed the subject.

Jayden let it go. "It was great growing up here. But it is a small town and everyone knows everybody, and everybody talks. Everyone will know you're here by the end of the day."

"I hope not." Chloe's blue eyes flashed terror before she masked them again.

"It's okay, Chloe."

"I'm not used to being the talk of the town, and would prefer not to be."

"Are you hiding?" Jayden was blunt. "I can protect you. But, you'd have to tell me what's going on."

"I'm not hiding. I just don't like to be the center of attention." Chloe played with her fork, avoiding eye contact with Jayden. "I just want to be someplace that I can just blend into the background and live a quiet life."

"You'll find a quiet life here, that's for sure. Although, for the first few days, you'll be the new topic of conversation, and then they will move on to the next thing that catches their eye." He sat back in his chair. His inquisitive stare made her feel so vulnerable and her valiant attempt to hide it was failing.

"Dinner was great. I owe you now for two meals." Chloe stood and collected the dirty dishes. Setting them on the counter, she turned the facet on to fill the sink. Her stomach churned and protested the dinner she had consumed. She closed her eyes and willed herself not to be sick. She didn't want to have to explain to Jayden.

"You okay?" Jayden shut off the water. She felt his hand on the small of her back.

"Yeah. Apparently I ate too fast."

"You're white. Come sit in the living room. I'll do the dishes."

"No. I'm okay. I can do them. Please, Jayden, you have done enough for me today." Chloe turned to face him. "Really, you must have other duties besides watching over the new girl in town. Thanks for dinner."

"Okay. I know when I'm being pushed out the door." Jayden smiled. "Get some rest. I'm sure I'll see you at the diner."

Chloe stood against the counter, watching him slip into his jacket. His eyes lingered on her face before he turned slowly and let himself out.

Turning back to the dishes, Chloe washed them as her mind replayed dinner. She felt a calmness about her when Jayden was close, but she couldn't forget that she had to keep her guard up at all times. It would be difficult to stay here because she relaxed too much. She must never allow herself to let down her guard and stop looking over her shoulder. Tony could not know where she was. She owed that much to herself and to the baby.

CHAPTER FIVE

A soft rap on the door brought Chloe's attention back to the present. She dried her hands on the blue dishtowel from one of the drawers and started towards the door. She peeked out the window, and saw Carla with her back to the door.

Pulling the door open, Chloe barely had time to step back when Carla turned and stepped through the door in one fluid motion it seemed. "Glad you're home. Wasn't sure if you had run out to explore or not." Carla glanced around the room.

"I haven't ventured out yet." Chloe wrapped the towel around her hand.

She moved towards the chair as Carla curled up on the couch. "Let's get to know each other." Carla grinned. "I loved to know all the news in town before anyone else."

"News? I'm not much news. Just a passerby who will work a few weeks to get some extra money." Chloe pulled her legs up in the chair.

Carla's soft eyes searched Chloe's face. "I understand. You don't know me. But I do hope to change that as you work for me."

"Anything special I need to wear?" Chloe hoped the change of conversation would go smoothly.

"No, whatever you're comfortable with. I have an extra apron at the diner that you can use."

"Thank you."

"I will let you get back to settling in. How about we ride together in the morning? No sense both of us taking cars."

"Sounds good." Chloe started for the door.

Carla pulled her into an impulsive hug. "See you tomorrow, five a.m."

"Okay." Chloe warmed with the afterglow of the hug. She hadn't had any girlfriends and certainly no acquaintances that would have just be impulsive like that.

* * *

Carla glanced back as she started down the stairs. Chloe had been quiet and very closed mouth about her past. Carla mentally berated herself for being too pushy. The poor girl had looked scared to death. She was skin and bones.

Jayden must've spent quite a bit of time here today. She had called the station to talk to him, and Betty informed her he was with the "new girl". For as long as Carla knew Jayden, he never had taken in interest so quickly in someone. Strolling across the lawn to the side door, Carla stopped here and there to deadhead the flowers in the flowerbeds along the house.

She threw the dry flower tops aside before swinging open the unlocked door. She had lived here her whole life, and her parents before her, and never once had she felt the need to lock up the house while they were gone.

Phone in hand, Carla punched out Jayden's home number. After four rings, she sighed and hung up. Where could he be? He had had dinner with Chloe.

Carla had a soft heart for anyone in trouble. She volunteered as much as she could at a home for battered women in the next town. She knew about living life in fear like those women did. She had seen fear flicker through Chloe's eyes though it was gone as quick as it was there. She knew there was more to the story and only hoped Chloe would trust her and Jayden to help with it.

Settling into the dark living room with a glass of wine, Carla closed her eyes and listened to the strains of Mozart fill the room. It was the way she relaxed every evening. It reminded her of the time she sat here, pregnant, waiting for her child to be born. Every night the ritual would take place for the baby to hear the music. Now it calmed her. She would need to go visit the grave of her baby daughter. Alive only a brief couple of hours, Carla had known the pain of losing half her heart when the baby's heart stopped beating. Nothing they could do. The doctors had been surprised the baby had even lived through the birth.

She sipped her wine. Tears rolled down her cheek unchecked with the memories assaulting her, the feel of the baby's tiny body in her arms. It wasn't healthy to sit here night after night with her pain. She knew that, but still couldn't resist the urge to put on the Mozart and listen. It was painful, yet calming.

CHAPTER SIX

Chloe tossed and turned all night. She was anxious about being at the diner tomorrow, interacting with so many strangers. Thoughts of being found out twisted through her mind. The need for safety plagued her. She needed to think of the baby before settling down--be sure Tony couldn't find her. Carla had brought to the surface feelings of family warmth that she had been missing for so many years.

At four a.m. she rose and showered. The water rain over her as her thoughts trailed off to Tony. She shivered despite the warmth of the water. He could find her if he wanted to. He had numerous resources at his disposal. She had shut off her cell phone with hopes that he couldn't trace her that way. She needed to trade it in for a new number. The question of how to hide her name around the cell phone swap plagued her.

As Chloe shut the water off, she reached for a towel with her free hand. Wrapped in terry, she wiped the moisture off the mirror. Big eyes stared back at her with dark circles encompassing them. She sighed and headed to the bedroom to find some make-up to conceal them. Dressed carefully in leggings and a long t-shirt, Chloe pulled her hair back in a ponytail. She slipped into a pair of light blue sneakers.

She turned in front of the full-length mirror. Her stature was thin, yet she wondered how long it would be before the pregnancy bump would show. She needed to leave before then. She couldn't tell Jayden of her situation. The thought of disappointing him overwhelmed her. Chloe couldn't afford to think of another man at this point in her life.

She slipped out the door. From the top step, she took in every car parked on the street. Nothing out of the ordinary.

"You're ready."

From below, Carla smiled up at her. Chloe hurried down the stairs with a wave. "Still getting used to the quietness."

"After you have been here a while you don't even notice it. More just take it for granted." Carla gestured towards her car. "I typically drive just because I'm exhausted by the time I close up."

"How long of a walk is it?" Chloe questioned out loud, although more to herself.

"About five minutes. Head toward the end of the street and turn right. The diner is a few blocks down."

"Do you mind if I walk?" Chloe moved a step from the car. The thought of checking out a bit of the town without anyone up and about was too enticing.

Carla shook her head. "Of course not. I'll see you there."

Chloe watched Carla's car round the corner and then started walking. The sound of the ocean was relaxing. Near the corner, the ocean spread out in front of her with mist rising. Her nerves calmed by the pounding waves and confidence increased with each step towards the diner. Tony wouldn't think to look in a small town for her. Her love for city life she had echoed more than once.

The bell over the door announced her arrival. The place was empty. The small diner was cozy. Following the long counter towards the back of the building, Chloe found Carla sifting through aprons.

"Voila! This one will be perfect for you." Carla pulled a small, bright blue one from the pile.

Chloe tied the apron behind her back while Carla reached for a fresh order pad. "Ever done this before?"

"Never." Chloe's voice trembled.

"Nothing to it. You write down what they want, and give it to Glenn, the cook in the kitchen. You keep the copy so you know what table the food goes to." Carla brushed off Chloe's apparent apprehension. "You'll be a pro in no time, and besides you will get to know the regulars."

Chloe jumped when the bell announced an arrival. Jayden ambled towards the bar. She slipped behind it, reaching for the coffeepot.

"Coffee?"

"Absolutely." Jayden glanced around at the empty diner. "Everyone decide to not show up this morning and take it easy on the new girl, Carla."

"Give her a break and behave yourself." Carla shook a finger at him.

"How's the slave driver?" Jayden turned his attention to Chloe who was fumbling to put the pot back.

"You're the first in, so it hasn't been bad yet."

Jayden winked. "You're in luck since I typically just have coffee in the morning." He drained half his cup before setting it down.

Chloe observed Carla filling sugar packets on each table. Glancing around she familiarized herself with the diner and where things were located.

"Need a refill, chief?" Chloe grabbed the coffeepot and waited for Jayden.

"Chief? That sounds a little formal." He held out his cup to be filled. "Please, call me Jayden."

She nodded as she put the pot back, needing some breathing room as heat coursed through her. The man filled out a uniform better than anyone she had seen before. Chloe had let her guard slip last night with the overwhelming comfortableness. With a sigh, she grabbed a couple of coffee cups and the pot again.

The diner filled up and the morning passed quickly. Chloe enjoyed the banter and comfortable conversation. Allowing herself to join in some of the joking, she was surprised when Carla told her to take a break before the lunch crowd hit.

Glenn placed a plate of pancakes and bacon in front of her. "I can't possibly,." Chloe said.

"Consider it a perk of working hard. Breakfast is on me." Carla waved the protest away. "Besides, you look like you're fading away to nothing."

Chloe couldn't deny the rumble coming from her stomach any longer. She drizzled maple syrup over the pancakes and dug in. The food disappeared quickly. Satisfied she wouldn't faint from hunger, Carla gave her the thumbs-up for getting back to work. Chloe kept pace well and was surprised when Carla told her to head for home at three p.m.

Pleased with herself for making it through the day, Chloe realized how tired she was. Without a protest, she headed to the door. The dazzle of the ocean across the street beckoned.

She stepped onto the beach and slipped off her sneakers. With her toes curled into the warm sand, Chloe closed her eyes and let the pounding waves take her away. Tension slipped from her shoulders as she realized how much she had been on edge. Allowing herself freedom to do something for herself, she made her way to the water's edge. The freezing temperature, although end of summer, stopped her from stepping into it. Maine's coastline never seemed to warm up.

The water teasing her every so often as she walked on the edge of the waves and her mind wander to her pregnancy. She had to find a doctor to start getting prenatal care. Finding a sheltered cluster of rocks, she made herself comfortable on the edge of one of them Her arms wrapped tight around her, the tears slipped from her eyes. The overwhelming feeling at the lack of family and support came over her. She wished her mom was here. Mom would have loved a grandchild and spoiled him or her rotten. Chloe sighed. She wanted her child to have the childhood she started to have and then missed out on —one full of love and warmth, comfort when needed and space to let grow when required. She wondered how she would know how to do all that when she hadn't had it herself.

"Chloe?"

She wiped her tears away before turning towards the voice. "Chief."

"Stop with the 'chief'. Are you okay?" Jayden leaned against the rock, looking out on the ocean.

"Fine. Just enjoying the view."

"I love it here. I can't imagine living anywhere without the ocean. How was the first day of work?"

"It was good," Chloe gushed. "I really enjoyed it. Carla is great."

"Her sentiments too." Jayden turned toward her. "Hungry?"

"A little, but more tired. I think I will head home and relax." Chloe stood and climbed off the rocks. "Thank you."

"For what?"

"Dinner last night...how kind you have been. Just wanted to be sure I told you in case I forgot."

"No need. I enjoyed your company. Want a ride home?"

"No, thanks." Chloe stepped away. "I think I'll walk."

She felt his eyes on her back as she moved towards the road, stopping only to slide her sneakers back on before heading up the street.

* * *

Jayden leaned against the rocks watching Chloe. He tried to ignore the disappointment that coursed through him. He had been up half the night searching for something that would give him insight to why she was running. Frustrated, he tossed and turned before giving into the longing to see her.

He returned to the diner. Carla would be the one who would know. She had a knack for spotting women in need and instinctively knew what the issue was. And knowing Carla, she had already become fast friends with Chloe. His fast pace spoke of his anxiousness to identify what was going on. He sensed a fear about Chloe.

Jayden pushed open the door and searched the room for Carla. The place had cleared out and only a few lingered over beverages. Just then, she pushed through the swinging doors from the kitchen.

"What's up, Jayden?" Carla slipped onto one of the barstools.

"Just curious to see how Chloe made out today." Jayden sat next to her.

"Let it go, Chief. She needs support and friendship right now, not an interrogation from you."

"I'm not going to interrogate her...just thought I could offer protection, if need be."

Carla paused, her eyes staring at Jayden. "Will you just trust me when I say she doesn't need you snooping?"

"What do you know?"

"Nothing, really. Just a hunch and some observations. I think she's running from someone who has hurt her. Don't know the story; just the look on her face at different times reminds me of the women at the shelter."

"Even more reason to protect her. We need to know what happened."

"No, Jayden. She needs to find herself. Don't ask questions. Let her learn to trust someone." Carla frowned. "Might be best if you just let me hang out with her and see if she will open up."

"You want me to stay away from her?"

"Somewhat, yes. Can you do that?"

Jayden closed his eyes and ran his hand along the stubble of his chin. "I guess."

"This isn't about your being attracted to her." Carla rested her hand on him arm. "I can't say it enough, if you want to protect her, let her be comfortable here."

"You've really taken a liking to her, haven't you?"

"Yes. She's sweet and so alone."

"I can't help but feel there is something more to her." Jayden sighed.

"Just be there for her. Really, Jayden, just be there."

CHAPTER SEVEN

Chloe strolled through the quiet streets, heading towards the library. It had been three days since she arrived in Arden. So far she was enjoying working at the diner and getting to know Carla. The large glass door swooshed open and she stepped inside, taking in the smell of paper and the wooden decor. Her eyes scanned the area in front of her. Bookshelves to the right housed fiction with a sign pointing to the back of the building for nonfiction. To the left, she spied the resource section with public computers. She settled in and brought up Google search. First looking for cell phone exchange information and local places to do so, she wrote everything down.

Turning her attention then to Tony, she ran his name but found nothing but business dealings, making him sound like quite the businessman. No criminal record to be found. A chill spread through her and she wrapped her arms around herself as she shivered. The screen cleared, she folded her notes and slipped them into her back pocket. She closed her eyes and allowed herself the luxury of imagining life in this town. It would be great for her child to grow up here. Not to mention living near Jayden. The chill left at the thought of Jayden and how friendly he had been. Had she misread his friendliness?

"Deep in thought?"

Chloe jumped up and turned.

"Hey, I'm sorry. I didn't mean to scare you." Jayden reached out, rested his hand on her arm. "You're shaking."

"I'm okay. You startled me." Chloe's voice shook as she attempted to brush off Jayden's hand causally.

She stepped backward and was brought up short by the chair. "I-I was just getting ready to leave. How long have you been standing there?"

"Just got here. Had to return a book and saw you. Thought I'd say hi."

Chloe pushed the chair firmly in and took a deep breath. *Calm yourself.* "I really have had a busy day and was just headed for the apartment."

"Want a ride?"

"No, I prefer to walk, really."

"May I walk with you?" He smiled as she searched his face.

"Sure." Chloe kept her face neutral. "What about your car?"

"I'll pick it up later. Your apartment isn't far. The exercise will do me good." He gestured her in front of him and stepped back so she could pass.

Walking in silence, Chloe's mind raced. What had he seen on the computer screen?

"Can I ask you something, Chloe?" Jayden slowed his pace.

"Of course." She stiffened her shoulders and braced for the worse.

"When are you going to settle down – make the apartment your own? You know, decorations, and all that. You didn't bring much with you."

"Well, I told you from the first day I wasn't staying long. No sense in decorating if I won't be here." Chloe shrugged, easing the tension. "Besides it's only been three days. I don't know many people starting over who move with a lot of stuff."

"You could stay." Jayden again reached for her arm. "Chloe, why not stay?"

"Jayden, I can't." Chloe stopped, but stared straight ahead. His touch made her tingle and the overwhelming sense of isolation hit her. A lone tear ran down her cheek. "I just can't. Please let it go."

"Chloe..."

She wiped the tear, and faced him. Her eyes locked with his and time seemed to stand still. "I need you to not ask, please."

"Okay, Chloe. I won't." He reached for her hands. "Please trust me though. I can help."

"There is nothing to help with, Jayden. Let it go." She squeezed his hands before pulling back. "Go get your car. I'm almost home. I'll walk the rest alone."

She briskly walked away. The tears flowed freely once she knew Jayden wasn't following. She felt his eyes on her and forced herself not to run. A tiny bit of sensibility tried to enter Chloe's head. This was not Tony. Jayden wasn't going to hurt her. Instinctively she knew that. Yet, her heart felt like it was tearing apart as she turned her back on him.

* * *

Jayden fought to keep his feet from running after her. He had pushed and had gone too far. Damn. He'd promised Carla to be cool. If she wouldn't talk to him, he would find out on his own.

He went back inside the library where the computer Chloe had been at was empty. He pulled up Chloe's latest search entry. Anthony Massey. Nothing spectacular about him. Jayden sat back wondering who he was. He wished he could do a background check for more than what the internet would show. Damn, privacy rules. In his gut he knew this person was the root of Chloe's fear, he just didn't know why.

Jayden shut down the computer after clearing the history, and headed outside. He sat in the car mulling over ideas rushing through his head. He started the engine and drove slowly towards her house, parking down the street, hidden in the shadows of the trees. He sat in the dark and watched, waiting, but not sure for what. The light in the apartment was muted by the shades pulled in the living room. No movement. The shadows deepened as Jayden sat there, unaware of the time passing.

Frustrated, he started the car and headed home. He hated the thought of leaving Chloe alone, but there was no reason to believe she was in danger. She was running, but from what?

His house was dark. Pulling in the driveway, he parked in front of the garage. On most days, he avoided being home as much as possible. The house was lonely and now, after meeting Chloe, it seemed oppressive to be here alone.

He stepped inside, picked up the mail from the foyer floor. It took only a minute to rifle through the bills and junk mail. He dumped it on the hallway desk and stepped into the kitchen to grab a beer. Jayden leaned against the counter. Time to develop a strategy to get through to Chloe.

She was attractive, although very thin, and he had the feeling beneath the cautious exterior was a free spirit just waiting to be set free. He had seen the pain while she talked about her parents and their deaths. She was young to have been through so much.

The phone shattered through his thoughts as it began to ring. Jayden pushed away from the counter and reached for the phone on the wall. He rolled his eyes as his sister's voice came through. He loved her dearly, but she could just talk forever.

"Hey, bro. What's up with the new girl?"

"What are you talking about?" Jayden sighed.

"I was talking with Betty. Apparently you are pretty taken with the new girl in town, a quiet little thing who's working at Carla's."

"You don't miss a trick, do you?" Jayden teased. "Maybe you should stop by Carla's and meet her. She doesn't know anyone in town yet."

"Am I supposed to be fishing for anything in particular?" Jayden heard the laughter in her voice.

"You know me too well, but no, just get to know her. I think she is running from something, running scared." Jayden paced the kitchen. "She needs a friend. You and Carla would be good for her."

"Another soul to save, Jayden...or is it more than that?"

"Just keeping the town safe."

"Bull. But I'll let that one go for now. Meet me for coffee in the morning and introduced me to her?"

"See you at seven." Jayden hung up before she could respond.

CHAPTER EIGHT

Chloe flipped pages in the book. Although the cover blurb was intriguing, she found it impossible to concentrate on the words. Her thoughts drifted to Jayden. She had been holding him at arm's length, but her heart was telling her to open up. What would it hurt to have an actual conversation with the man? Instinctively she knew he would never physically hurt her.

She had never felt so connected to someone so quickly. A slight rap at the door brought a sigh of relief. She looked through the peephole and saw Jayden. Her breath caught and she swallowed hard. It was one thing to daydream about, another to spend time in his company.

Chloe pulled open the door. "Hi."

"Hi. Were you busy?"

She gestured for him to enter. "Just reading."

Jayden picked up her book and skimmed the back. "Any good?"

"Honestly, I wasn't really getting into it." Chloe slipped on the couch and curled her legs under her. "What's up?"

"I was feeling a bit restless and thought you might like some company." He leaned back on the couch and stretched out his legs.

Chloe pulled her knees up. "Tell me about growing up here. I hear it gets pretty quiet in the off season."

"Yeah, it does. When we were kids I couldn't wait to get out of here. I wanted to see the world, do something exciting."

"Did you? Go see the world?"

Jayden shook his head. "No. Got as far as Portland. Loved the 'big city', but life changes."

They fell into a comfortable silence. Chloe agonized how much she never got a chance to do anything.

Jayden broke the silence. "How about you? Any big dreams you followed through on?"

"No. Unfortunately, like you said, life got in the way."

"What were your dreams?"

Chloe sighed. "When I was younger, I wanted to dance. Mom signed me up for ballet classes and I danced until I was ten. Then Dad lost his job and they couldn't afford it anymore."

"Any other dreams after that?"

"I wanted to be a nurse when I got into high school." Chloe paused, biting her lower lip.

"What happened?"

"Life. My parents were killed in a car accident when I was sixteen. Everything changed for me." Chloe held her legs tightly, fighting the tears.

"I'm sorry, Chloe."

She smiled. "Thanks. You learn to live the life you've been given. We can't all have a happy ending."

"You can make your own happy ending." Jayden turned towards her. "What happened after your parents died?"

"Over the next two years, until I turned eighteen, I was in and out of foster homes. Apparently I was too sullen and no one wanted me around."

"Sullen? You had lost your parents. How about sad, frightened, needing reassurance?"

Chloe let out a small laugh. "Yeah. How about those? Unfortunately, there are a lot of people that take in foster kids for the money, not because they care about the kids."

Jayden shook his head. "What a shame."

"I often wondered how different my life would've been if someone had just cared. Moot point though." She shrugged.

"What happened when you turned eighteen?"

"I stayed with friends here and there, got a job hoping to save enough money for my own place."

"Chloe..."

She held up her hand. "Don't you dare feel sorry for me."

"I don't feel sorry for you, but no one should go through that. You were just a kid."

"It's life. There are a lot of teens out there in the same boat. You must have seen it working in Portland."

"Yes, too much of it. It always hits you a little harder when you hear firsthand about it instead of seeing it from a distance."

"Someday I want to have foster kids. Give them the home they really deserve."

"What about nursing? It's not too late to go back to school."

Chloe shook her head. "Maybe not too late, but not feasible at the moment." She closed her eyes and let her mind drift to thoughts of Tony and how much being with him had affected her life, and her opportunities to better herself. She didn't want to admit it, but she had made a bad decision and it was going to cause consequences for the rest of her life. If she ever could get back on her feet, would she ever have the courage to make something of her life? Even for her child?

"How did you get mixed up with this guy?" The sound of Jayden's voice brought her back to the present.

"Tony. I was alone, nowhere to go and he showed an interest in me. Sounds pathetic now, but at the time I just wanted someone to love me."

"Doesn't sound pathetic. How long were you together?"

"Five years. At first he was great." She blinked to keep the tears from falling. "After awhile you suddenly realize how alone you really are. Somehow he had convinced me to sever ties with my friends. When things got really bad, I had no one to turn to for help."

"There's always help, Chloe. There are so many agencies that help women involved in domestic abuse."

"Maybe, but fear plays a huge role in stopping you from getting out."

"I'm so sorry you went through that."

Chloe shrugged. "It's life."

Jayden sat up straight. "You have to know it's not life. It's not the way it should be, and it's not your fault."

She gave him a thin smile. "Those are easy words to say when you've never been there."

A heavy silence fell between them and she took a deep breath as Jaden stood.

"Well, I should be going. Thanks for the company, I enjoyed it."

Chloe nodded as sadness filled her. Jayden left and she was overwhelmed with loneliness. She longed for more conversations like that with him, but she needed to not let herself fall for him. She had to hold him at arm's length.

CHAPTER NINE

The phone was ringing at the diner when Chloe entered. No patrons were in sight and Carla was nowhere to be seen. She froze, uncertainty making her heart thump in her chest, the rush of blood causing a roar in her ears. She stood still until the phone was silent before starting her morning ritual of refilling sugar holders on each table.

Chloe had spent the night in fitful sleeping stages plagued by nightmares that Tony had found her. She awoke this morning in a cold sweat with a sense of dread looming over her. She had packed up her clothes and drove to the diner this morning with every intention of moving on as soon as her shift was over. The tip money from today would have to last for gas and a few groceries.

"You okay, honey?" Carla's eyes were full of concern.

"I'm okay, just a long night." Chloe focused on her tasks, avoiding eye contact.

"Come on over here for a second, Chloe." Carla poured a glass of milk and placed it on the counter, pushing it towards Chloe as she sat down.

"What's that for?"

"Strength. Honey, you are going to have to get some medical attention soon."

"What do you mean?" Chloe's hand instantly rested on her stomach.

"Yes, I can tell. No, others don't know, but I have been there myself, pregnant, alone and hoping no one would find out." Carla walked around the counter and slid into a stool next to Chloe. "You want to talk about it?"

"I thought no one would know for a while and that I would have time to find someplace to settle down before..."

"I think you have found that place, Chloe. Look around you. You fit right in here and whatever, or whoever, you are running from, you're safe."

Chloe fidgeted and played with the glass. "I don't know, Carla. You don't understand."

"Okay. How about you do me a favor after work? I could use some help dropping off some supplies to a place I help out at once in a while."

"I can do that, but not for long." Chloe lifted her tear-filled eyes to meet Carla's. "I'm leaving tonight."

"Let's see what happens when the day ends and our errands are finished. I think you might be surprised." Carla patted her hand as she started for the kitchen. "Just let yourself enjoy the customers today."

Chloe took her glass and placed it in the bus bin. Uncertainty pressed down on her as she questioned how Carla knew. She couldn't bear it if Carla told Jayden.

Chloe worked hard the first hour of work, the regular customers were in and kept her smiling. She was startled when Jayden arrived in the doorway with a beautiful girl. Ducking into the kitchen, Chloe breathed in deeply to calm the fluttering of her heart. How did he have that effect on her?

She glanced out the kitchen door. Carla was standing next to a booth chatting with Jayden and the woman. Chloe envied her long black hair. She sighed as she ran her hand through her ponytail. She would never look that glamorous. Pen and order pad in hand, she walked slowly over to the booth.

"Chloe, this is Jayden's sister, Jocelyn. Joce. Chloe, my new lifesaver." Carla squeezed Chloe's elbow.

"Nice to meet you, Chloe." Jocelyn extended her hand. "I understand you have been keeping my brother busy."

"Nice to meet you. What can I get you?" She ignored the implication of time spent with Jayden.

"Just coffee for me this morning."

"Okay." Chloe glanced quickly at Jayden. "How about you, Jayden?"

"Coffee for me too."

Work flew by and Chloe dreaded seeing the clock turn to three. It had been a busy day and tips were good. Uneasiness settled on her as she counted her money, knowing she wasn't coming back again. She should have said something to Jayden, but he would have tried to convince her to stay.

She regretted her promise to go with Carla, not knowing where they were headed. Chloe just wanted to reveal everything to her and see where things went, but fear kept her mouth shut.

"Ready?" Carla held the kitchen door open. "We can leave your car here and come back for it later."

"Okay. Where are we headed?" Chloe pocket her tips and grabbed her purse.

"I want to share something with you—you'll see when we get there." Carla picked up the box of food Glenn had prepared earlier. "Only about a fifteen minute ride. We won't be gone long."

They drove in silence, listening to the soft rock that Carla had turned up. The scenery went by in a blur, searching her mind for answers on what to do.

"We're here." Carla's voice was soft. They sat in front of an old Victorian house in need of paint.

"Who lives here?"

The privet hedges were overgrown and they almost hid the beautiful wraparound porch.

"Some friends of mine. Come on, grab those bags in the back seat."

Chloe reached for the bags while Carla headed up the stairs. She started slowly after her, eyes roaming over everything in sight, taking it all in.

"What is this place?" Chloe whispered, standing behind Carla at the door.

"A place for women. I drop off food once a week for them to help out."

A young woman in her early thirties opened the door. "Carla, come on in."

"Hi, Sarah. This is my friend, Chloe." Carla handed the box of food off to Sarah and turned to grab the bag from Chloe.

"Nice to meet you." Sarah nodded towards the back of the house. "Come on, the rest are in the kitchen."

Chloe glanced around the house as they passed down the hallway to the kitchen. It was old, but nicely furnished. There appeared to be two bedrooms off the living room, a bath, and the kitchen on the main floor.

"Are you joining us, Chloe?" Sarah had her back to her, unpacking the box.

"Joining you? I'm just helping Carla today." Chloe stepped back, leaning against the doorframe.

"Chloe has been working for me, new to the area." Carla gestured around the room. "This is the rest of the gang: Mindy, Deb, Rachel and Melissa."

"Hi." Chloe took in each one of them. They seemed comfortable, yet on guard. She wondered how they all came to be together.

"Chloe, this house is a safe home for battered women."

"Really, How is it safe, and how did you guys find out about it?"

"We have contacts all around, in hospitals, different places women would come in contact with. Battered women aren't always up front about what is going on, feeling it is their fault, or that there's no way out. We help them. Once they feel safe with us, we help them get away and start over."

"All of you are from violent homes?" Chloe, eyes wide with wonder, carefully masking her fear.

"Most of us." Sarah gestured for Chloe to join them at the table and waited while she slowly made her way over to sit gingerly on a chair. "Mindy's boyfriend beat her whenever he could. The others have had husbands that were unstable and violent, so it was more of a sporadic abuse. I have been here the longest and seem to be the house mom, settling everyone in and staying after everyone is gone. It gives me a purpose now that my kids are grown."

"And they never find you?"

"No one ever has. We have been able to swap out cell phones for new ones. A few of us have changed our last names to help feel safer, but overall we have very good friends looking out for us." Sarah reached out a hand and grasped Chloe's. "Jayden checks up on us and the local chief watches over us daily."

"I can't imagine living that way." Chloe's voice was soft.

"Can't you?" Carla's voice was low. "Isn't that what you are doing now? Except you feel you can't trust anyone and that you think no one knows you are running?"

"I'm not running, Carla." A lone tear ran down Chloe's cheek. "I-I'm just trying to find a place to start over."

"What happened to make you want to start over, Chloe?" Melissa asked.

"Nothing. Lost my parents years ago, just have been looking for something since then."

"Do you have a boyfriend?" Sarah asked.

"No! I mean, I used to, but Tony and I broke up." Chloe stood. "I really need to get going, Carla."

"Okay. I will see you girls next week." Carla gave hugs to everyone as Chloe edged towards the door.

"Nice to meet you. I'll be in the car, Carla." Chloe was at the front door before anyone could answer.

Carla started the car and turned towards Chloe. "Do you need anything before we head back?"

"I don't think so." Chloe avoided eye contact.

"Do you have a cell phone?"

"Yeah, but..." Chloe folded her hands in her lap. "I just don't use it much."

"How about stopping by the store I use all the time and getting a new one, new number? You don't have to give out the number, but I would like it so I can keep in touch."

Chloe faced Carla. "I don't know what you're thinking, but I'm just fine." She snapped at her friend and it left a hollow feeling in her stomach.

"I never said you weren't. I simply asked if you wanted to swap out your cell phone." Carla put the car in Drive and pulled out.

"I guess that would be okay." Chloe stared out the window. "I don't know where I'm going."

"I figured as much. Have you thought about how you are going to get prenatal care for your baby?"

"No."

"You need to start thinking of that. Is there really any reason you can't stay with me in the apartment, for a while longer?"

Chloe sighed. "I don't think I should."

"At least stay another night and maybe we can look at some maps and figure out where you want to head to. I don't want you to leave not knowing where you are going."

"Why does it matter?"

"Maybe a see a bit of me in you and I can relate. Why are you running? And don't say you're not. I can see the fear in your eyes." Carla paused. "I remember wishing I had someone I could have turned to for help when I was going through it. I guess I want to make sure you know you have someone to talk to."

"Why did you have to be so nice to me? I should have just kept going that first day." Chloe bit her lip fighting back the tears that threatened to destroy what little strength she had left..

Carla maneuvered the car into a parking spot next to a cell phone store. "Let's get you a phone. Do you have your old one with you?"

"Yes." Chloe exited the vehicle and looked around. The storefront advertised cell phones, but no specific carrier.

"Let's go." Carla held open the door. "Is the cell phone in your name?"

"No. And I haven't turned it on since I left." Chloe handed it to her.

While Carla went to the counter and talked with an elderly gentleman, she browsed around the store, keeping her eyes on Carla and the gentleman. Her cell phone was handed over the counter. Carla motioned her to come close.

"Any contacts you need transferred?"

"No. There really isn't anything in there." Chloe fidgeted.

"Okay, we'll take the usual, Bob." Carla glanced at Chloe. "Basic phone, not a lot of bells and whistles, but totally untraceable."

Chloe was speechless as Bob brought out the phone and activated it. Within minutes they were out of the store and she was ready to go..

CHAPTER TEN

Chloe sat in the apartment with the lights off. She had a phone, her bag was packed, and yet she had allowed Carla to talk her into staying another night. A strange prickling started at the base of her neck. The same feeling she used to get when Tony was watching her. She went to the window, stood behind the curtain and peeked out. The street was dark. No one around her car.

She shrugged and turned when she saw a shadow. Someone was out there. Reaching for her cell phone, she typed in Carla's number. With finger poised over the Send button, she strained her eyes to focus in the dark, trying to see the shadow. Headlights coming down the road illuminated a person standing across the street, but he slipped backwards, out of the light.

The car parked behind hers, and out stepped Jayden. A sense of relief flooded Chloe yet she resisted the temptation to run to the door. She stood beside the window watching him cross the lawn to the stairs to the apartment. She turned her eyes to the shadow again. He was still there. Her heart raced in her chest as her eyes strained to focus. He couldn't have found her, he just couldn't have. She thought she was safe. Now, not only was she in jeopardy, but she had put Carla there too.

She jumped as someone knocked on the door. Glancing out the door side window, she threw open the door, reached for Jayden's hand, pulling him in.

"What's going on, Chloe?"

"There's someone watching the apartment, in the shadows." Her voice trembled. "Please believe me."

"I believe you." Jayden crossed to the window and looked out. The street was empty. "I don't see anyone."

Chloe moved beside him and viewed the street. Her eyes strained to see through every shadow, but the prickling was gone. He had left. "He'll be back."

She moved to the couch and sank into the cushion with a sigh. As she stared at the carpet her mind raced to sort out the day's happenings. Should she ask Carla to stay at the home with the other women? Her first desire was to protect her baby. He couldn't know she was pregnant.

"Chloe?" Jayden's soft voice penetrated her thoughts as he sat next to her. His arm went around her shoulders as he pulled her close. "Talk to me."

She closed her eyes and leaned against him, washed by the safety of his arms. The tension left her shoulders as the tears flowed. She sobbed and heard his murmurings into her hair as he held her.

Pushing away, she stood. "I have to leave."

"What's going on Chloe? I can protect you if someone is after you." He reached for her hand and she slipped out of reach.

"I just can't, Jayden. It's not fair to you."

She turned towards the window, but stayed to the side. Looking out, she wiped the tears from her eyes. A sense of urgency overcame her. She sighed as Jayden came behind her and wrapped his arms around her. She leaned back against him and the longing for safety battled against the need to leave.

She closed her eyes as he kissed her neck. "Stay with me, Chloe."

Turning to face him, she searched his eyes. "I..." She never got the words out as his mouth covered her, caressing her, reassuring her. She melted into his touch and her body responded as her mind screamed *No!* Her hands wandered up his shoulders to the back of his neck. Fingers entwined in his hair, the urgency to feel him closer brought her to press against him.

"I'm sorry." Jayden backed off and struggled to compose himself.

"I'm not, but it doesn't change the fact I have to leave." Chloe moved to the couch. "I need to get out of here, far away." She sighed. "If he's out there he will find me again."

"What are you running from?"

A knock at the door startled them. Jayden inched towards the handle as Chloe raced down the hall for the bathroom. Slipping the door shut behind her all but a crack; she heard Carla's voice speaking softly. Unable to make out the words, she allowed her mind to wander to the "what if's" in her life.

"Chloe?" Carla tapped on the bathroom door. "Are you okay?"

Chloe released the grip she had on the handle and the door opened, . She dropped into Carla's arms and hugged her tight. "I'm fine. But I should have left this afternoon."

"Jayden said there was someone outside. Come stay at my place tonight."

She shook her head no and went to the living room. "I don't want you getting in the middle of this."

"Come stay at my place. No one will bother you if you are with the chief of police," Jayden offered.

"I need to get away from here." Chloe paced the living room.

"You need to think this through." Carla's protective tone brought Chloe's thoughts to the baby. "You can't run forever. At some point you need to think of what is the best thing."

"I know," Chloe whispered. She glanced at Jayden and was relieved to see he didn't seem to be aware of the hidden message Carla was sending.

"We can get you to a safe house, if you want."

"No. There is no need." Chloe bit her lower lip, deep in thought.

"Okay, then. I will stay here tonight so Chloe can get some sleep. We will decide over breakfast what will be done." Jayden's commanding tone startled Chloe.

"Don't think you can decide what's best for me."

"I didn't mean anything by it, but right now you are too tired to think straight. You need some sleep." Jayden nudged her towards the bedroom. "Go, get some sleep. I will be right here on the couch if you need anything."

She slipped into the bedroom longing for Jayden to join her and hold her through the night.

* * *

With Chloe gone from the living room, Jayden positioned himself near the window. He had a clear view of most of the street, including Chloe's car. "What is going on with her?" He never looked at Carla, but felt her eyes staring at him.

"I have no idea."

"Give me a little credit, Carla. You got her a new cell phone and took her to the safe house today. There had to be a reason and I want to know what I'm dealing with."

"I don't know. It's a conversation you need to have with her."

"Aren't you the one who told me not to ask?" Jayden suddenly stared at Carla, trying to read her face.

"Yes, but that was before I knew she was planning on leaving. We can't let her go now." Carla's tone held urgency and fear to it.

Jayden canvassed the area outside the house with his eyes. No unusual shadows or cars on the road.

"Go home, Carla, and lock your doors tonight." Jayden's tone held no room for argument.

"Keep her safe, Jayden," Carla whispered as she started down the stairs.

* * *

Joe shrank back behind the trees. Pulling out a cell phone, he punched the number he knew by heart. There wasn't much time if she sensed she was being watched. He rambled off Jayden's license plate with explicit instructions to get the information back to him ASAP. He wasn't about to let his boss know there was another man with her until he had full information. He had already researched the woman from the diner. She could be trouble at some point. Right now, he hoped to slip in and grab Chloe before anyone saw. This man would be a problem if he didn't leave. He hated leaving lose ends, but hated even more being forced into violence.

Walking around the back of the house, he stopped every so often staring at windows and doors. He hadn't expected her to be involved with someone so quick. Boss wouldn't be happy about that. Stairs led to a deck outside the apartment. In a better position to watch, he shrank into shadows and settled in. It was going to be a long night.

CHAPTER ELEVEN

Jayden glanced down at his watch, two a.m. He'd been staring out the window for two hours and nothing. But the fear in Chloe's eyes was real. He pulled the curtains shut and laid back on the couch. He closed his eyes, but his mind was running in all directions trying to figure out what was going on. He played different scenarios and yet couldn't put a finger on what might be bothering her.

He heard the bedroom door open and sat up. "Chloe?"

"Yes. I couldn't sleep." She padded into the living room and sank into the chair, tucking her feet under her. "Did I wake you?"

"No, not at all." She was sitting in the shadows just out of the beam of moonlight. He couldn't read her face. "Do you want to tell me what's going on now?"

The silence was deafening as Jayden waited for Chloe to speak. Her fingers picked at imaginary lint on her yoga pants. It seemed like forever before she cleared her throat.

"I don't know where to start. I didn't mean to bring trouble with me here." She paused, glancing up to the window. "I'm sorry."

"Chloe, there is nothing to be sorry about, but let us help you." Jayden felt a desperation; he was torn between wanting to help and protect her, and the fear of not being able to because of his own demons.

"I was living with my boyfriend, Tony. It wasn't a good relationship." She let the words hang in the air.

"Was he abusive?" Jayden's hand clenched into a fist at the thought of someone hurting her.

"Yes." The word was barely a whisper. "I needed to get away so I left in the night while he was gone."

Jayden processed her words. In his gut he knew there was more to it, but didn't press. "And you drove all night and that's when I found you?"

"Yes." Chloe's feet slipped across the floor and she sat in the chair and leaned forward. Resting her elbows on her knees. "I wasn't going to stay here. I was going to keep going, but I got comfortable. I like working with Carla and—"

"You don't have to run. Give me his name. Make a report of abuse and let me run a background check to see what we are dealing with."

"Anthony Massey, but I won't sign a complaint."

"Why? Is there anything else I should know?" Jayden held his breath.

"No. That's it." The lie made her tremble. She couldn't tell him about the pregnancy. He would walk out the door and she would never see him again.

Jayden looked at his watch. Two-thirty. They still had a while before daylight. He stood and went to the kitchen and looked out the back door window. He saw nothing, but his gut told him whoever was looking for Chloe wasn't far away.

"Jayden?"

He turned at the soft voice behind him. "I don't see anyone, but I believe you that someone was."

"I don't want to run, but I can't stay here and put Carla or you in danger." Her voice trembled and she bit down on her bottom lip.

Jayden closed the gap between them and pulled her close. "You don't have to run. We can get you to the safe house until this is cleared up. My hands are tied, police-wise to protect you without a formal complaint, though." He kissed the top of her head and held her tight.

"If he found me here, he will find me there, too."

"Then let me stay here and protect you. Maybe we can confront them."

She shuddered in his arms and looked up at him. Her eyes wide as she shook her head no. She closed her eyes. Jayden's lips gently touched hers. She sighed as she wrapped her arms around his neck and leaned into the kiss.

A tapping at the door brought them apart. Jayden moved to the front door and glanced out the window. Carla stood there.

Jayden pulled open the door and jerked her inside. "What are you doing?"

"I couldn't sleep and thought maybe Chloe was awake. I don't see anyone outside. Do you think they're gone?" Carla paused as Chloe moved into the living room.

"I couldn't sleep either." She sank into the chair.

Carla plopped into the corner of the couch. "So what do you want to do?"

* * *

Chloe gave her a small smile. "I told Jayden about Tony." She gave Carla a small shake of her head, conveying no to the question in Carla's eyes that she only assumed was regarding the pregnancy. "I don't know what to do."

Carla rested her chin in her hands. "You know you can go to the shelter?"

"I don't want Tony showing up there. Those women feel safe now, how can I bring trouble into their lives?"

"Chloe, they knew when they met you that you were being abused. They know how to help." Carla reached out and took both Chloe's hands. "Let us help you."

Chloe realized Jayden was watching her. Defeat hit her. She couldn't save herself or her baby in this mess. She longed to have all this behind her and just be able to rest in his strength.

"I'll go to the shelter." She stood up. "When is the safest time?"

Carla stood. "I would think now, in the night is the best. Jayden?"

Jayden moved to the window and looked out into the street again. "Let's move now. It should be easy to tell if someone follows us."

Chloe had already carried her suitcase to the door. "Let's do this before I lose my nerve." She rolled her shoulders to relieve tension.

Jayden placed his hand on her back as he picked up the suitcase. "Let me get this in the car and then I'll come back for you."

She nodded. "Carla, are you coming too?"

"Absolutely. Go ahead, Jayden. We'll all go down together." Carla grabbed the extra key to the deadbolt and locked the door. Jayden and Chloe were just about to the car when Carla hit the bottom of the stairs. She glanced over her shoulder and saw nothing but darkness. A chill ran up her spine and the hairs on her neck stood up. Someone was there; she just knew it.

Carla sprinted to the car as Jayden shut Chloe's door and moved to the driver's side. "Move, Jayden. Someone's behind the house."

Jayden slid in as Carla jumped in the back. The tires squealed and the car whipped around the corner before either of us were buckled in. Jayden drove in the opposite direction of the safe house until he was sure no one was following, and then circled around to come up behind the house where the car couldn't be seen from the street. Carla had called ahead and told Sarah they were on the way.

Chloe's heart pounded in her head as they drove through the darkened streets. She dropped her head back against the cold leather seat had closed her eyes as exhaustion overtook her and drifted off. She woke in a start, drenched with sweat. She rubbed her eyes to block back the nightmare that haunted her.. "Hey, we're here. Carla took your bag in."

"Okay." She shook her head to clear the fog. "I didn't realize I was that tired." Her voice trembled as she swung her legs out of the car.

"Come on. Let's get you inside and then you can rest." Jayden kept his arm around her until they were safely in the kitchen where Sarah and Carla were talking.

Sarah put an arm around Chloe's shoulders. "Let's get you settled in your room and you can get some sleep. You are perfectly safe here. Sleep as long as you want in the morning." She quickly moved Chloe through the house into a small bedroom on the second floor. "My room is right across the hall if you need anything."

Chloe just nodded and walked into the room. There was a small light on a nightstand. A blue quilt had been pulled back invitingly. Chloe slid under the covers and pulled them up under her chin. Within minutes she was asleep.

* * *

Jayden sat in the kitchen with Carla when Sarah entered. "She's already dozed off. She must be exhausted."

"We don't know much about her," Jayden explained. "All we have is the name of her abuser and that someone has found her at Carla's."

"I gave you all the information I have," Carla interrupted.

Sarah nodded. "She isn't saying much, huh?"

"No." Jayden ran his fingers through his hair. "I just want to help her. Why won't she let us?"

Sarah leaned back in her chair. "I would say she has taken a huge step in that direction – she's here. Jayden, you have to remember on that side of the abuse, you don't know who to trust. Give her time."

CHAPTER TWELVE

Jayden took Carla back to her house at daybreak. Carla reached for the door handle, but turned to face Jayden. "Give her time, Jayden. She told you about the abuse. Just look into that guy and stop him from hurting her again."

"There's more to it, isn't there?" Jayden searched Carla's face. "I can't do anything without her wanting the help."

Carla shook her head. "I don't know what more there is than she told you, but give her a chance to trust you. Don't bully her about it."

"I'm not a bully."

Carla smiled. "No, not a bully, just like a dog with a bone."

She got out of the car and glanced around. She waved to Jayden as he drove off. She headed inside to get ready for work. It was going to be a long day.

* * *

Joe watched from the back of the house. He didn't know where they had taken Chloe, but Tony was on the way, furious that there had been another man with her. He still didn't know if the man was involved with her or with the other woman. He had broken into the Chloe's apartment when they had left and found nothing. Not even a trace she had been there. Obviously, Chloe had gotten good at hiding things from Tony. Women had come and gone before, but they always returned to Tony knowing they couldn't make it on their own.

His phone vibrated in his pocket. Six a.m. Time to face the music. Tony's name appeared on the caller ID. "Yeah, boss."

"Tell me you have her." The force of the words made him pull the phone back from his ear.

"She left in the night with another couple. I don't know where they went. My vehicle wasn't here so I couldn't follow them. There's no trace of her in the apartment."

"I'm surrounded by incompetence." The silence that followed was deafening.

"What do you want me to do?"

A deep sigh rang over the phone. "Get to the diner and do some digging. Find some answers for me before I arrive. I will meet you there in two hours." The phone went silent. Two hours didn't give him much time. He skirted around the back of the house to head towards the beach without Carla seeing him.

The diner opened in an hour, which only gave him an hour to get some information. He needed to find out the man's identity before Tony arrived. How he hoped it was someone they could intimidate without hurting. Tony always went above and beyond what needed to be done.

In the diner, he chose a seat in the back where he could see the door. The girl from last night approached carrying a coffeepot.

"Coffee?"

"Yes, please." He moved the cup closer to her.

"New to this area?"

"Just passing through. This town reminded me of a little one I used to go to as a child and thought it would be a great place to try. What do you recommend?"

"House special has eggs, pancakes, bacon or sausage and home fries."

"Sounds good. Are you the only one working?"

Carla studied him a moment. "I'm the owner and yes, sole worker besides the cook."

"Must keep you hopping." He smiled.

"I'll get your order right in." She turned as Jayden walked in. Pouring him a cup of coffee at the bar, she moved to the kitchen to place the order.

The man at the bar—that was the guy from last night. Damn, a cop. That was all Tony needed.

Carla moved to the counter and talked softly with him. He couldn't make out the words, but he saw her glance at him a couple of times. He needed to keep his cover and not alarm them. He heard "order up" from the kitchen. Carla returned with his food.

"Enjoy. Need more coffee?"

"Yes, please. This looks delicious." He held the cup as she filled it.

"Thanks. Just signal if you need anything else." She walked away.

The hour flew by. The diner filled and stayed full as the locals chatted away with each other. He figured this must be the local hangout. He didn't see Chloe and by the owner's admission she was the only one working, although people were asking for 'the new girl'. Where had they taken her?

The street door opened. Tony filled the door with his broad shoulders. He raised his hand slightly to catch Tony's attention.

Tony slid into the bench seat; he wasted no time. "What did you find out?"

"Not much. All I know is the owner of the diner and the cop over there were the two that snuck Chloe off last night."

"The cop? Geeze, give me a break. How did she get mixed up with a cop?"

"I'm not sure." He sat back and waited. Tony was too calm about all this. He never held his temper, didn't matter if he was in a crowd or not. He wondered what Tony had up his sleeve. Did he know more about this town and why Chloe came here?

Carla showed up at their table with the coffeepot. "Coffee?"

"Yes." Tony looked her up and down.

"Did you want to order?" Carla's voice was cold in response to Tony's obvious boldness.

"I'll have what he had." Tony smirked. "Unless you're offering anything else?"

"If you are interested in something else, my suggestion would be for you to walk right back out that door." She turned and went to the kitchen to put the order in.

Tony chuckled. "She's a feisty one." They saw the cop looking over at them with interest. "Maybe it's time to make nice with the officer."

* * *

Tony stood and sauntered across the diner. "Nice place you have here. I'm looking for some possible local work, anything really. Maybe you know of something, officer."

The cop gave him the once-over. "Nope, no work this time of year around here. I would head for the city. They might have something." Jayden said as he turned away Tony, dismissing him.

Tony clenched his hands at his side. No one ever dismissed him. He may be a cop, but Tony outweighed him and could take him down before he knew what hit him. He glanced around. All the locals were watching. He turned and walked back to the table.

"Not a friendly bunch around here." Tony sat back with his arm resting across the back of the bench.

Carla slid the plate in front of him and placed the check on the table. "Enjoy." She walked off without waiting for a response or asking if they needed anything else.

Her hips swayed as she moved across the room. "That woman needs to be taken down a notch," he muttered.

"Probably ought to keep a low profile, boss. We don't want trouble before we find Chloe." Said Joe.

"Which was your job and you've blown it. If you wanted to keep a low profile you should have snatched her last night before her cavalry rushed in to save her."

* * *

Tony finished his meal and pushed the plate aside. "What's your plan, since you seem to have everything so in control here?"

"I don't have one. The locals are close-mouthed. The owner states she is the only one that works here, yet I saw Chloe working the other day."

"Why did you wait so long to try and grab her?"

"Boss, she hasn't been alone. She was with the owner all the time. I don't think she has told them about you, but that cop has a thing for her. That's obvious."

"Really? Maybe I should have another chat with him. Let's see how pretty boy holds up under some questioning." Tony sipped his coffee.

"You don't want to do that. Come on, keep a low profile until we have more information."

"Always trying to be the pleaser. Maybe you aren't cut out for this type of work, Joe." Tony watched his expression. Joe's face whitened a shade and shook his head.

"I have it under control. Give me another couple of days."

"Don't have a couple of days. You've got 24 hours and then I'm taking it into my own hands. Got it?"

"Yes." Joe stood up and threw some money on the table. "Let's get out of here."

* * *

Jayden watched the two men leave the building. He turned to Carla. "I'm headed back to the station to do a little digging into this Anthony that Chloe was talking about. Do you think one of those two was him?"

"Possibly. My guess is it's the one who talked to you. He would be that ballsy." Carla gave Jayden a quick hug. "Be careful."

"Same to you. Call if you need anything."

Jayden walked outside. The two were nowhere in sight. He slid into the cruiser and turned toward the station. He needed to do a background check and get some photos of this guy so he would know who he was dealing with. Without a formal complaint on this man, he would have to do it without the criminal database. Dread clenched in his stomach at the thought of Chloe being in danger. Would he be able to step up and save her if push came to shove? The image of a boy crumbling in front of him when Jayden had shot at a robber popped into his mind. The boy came out of nowhere. Jayden wipes the sweat from his forehead as the nightmare re-played in his head. He had been cleared of any wrongful actions, but had left the force in Portland at that point and had run home to hide from the dreadful memories. His dad had talked him into taking the chief of police job shortly before he died. Crime was rare here in Arden. Yet in the back of his mind, the fear of not being able to ever draw his gun again plagued him. In the past four years, he had grown accustomed to the small easygoing town. Little by little the memory of that horrific night where a young boy had died in his arms had faded. But not gone away.

He shook off the memories as he walked into the station. The scent of a fresh pot of coffee hit him and he grabbed cup. He closed his office door. He didn't want to be disturbed on this inquiry and wanted to shield Chloe at all cost from locals talking about her.

He opened his computer and sent a quick email off to his private investigator friend in Portland, telling him briefly about Chloe and the urgency of what was going on.

Jayden pulled up Google and searched for Tony. He found nothing, just like at the library. This man either was living under an alias or had a really good friend who could make his life invisible. He prayed his PI friend could dig up something to use as leverage.

As he sat back, his thoughts drifted to Chloe. There was more to the story, he just knew deep in his gut. But the fear in her eyes terrified him from pushing her any further. It had taken a lot of courage on her part to accept their help. She was in good hands with Sarah. The chances of her being found were slim. His heart ached for her. All he could think of was *I can't lose her.* Where had those thoughts come from? He had held back from any relationships since the shooting. He couldn't bring another into his nightmare that he lived with every day. Yet, something about Chloe had him wanting more. Wanting love, a family.

Jayden startled as a tone from the computer indicated a new email. The PI had sent a quick message. *We need to talk in person. Bad news on this guy. When and where?*

Jayden reached for the phone and punched in the number. He spoke as soon as the phone was answered: "How soon can you get here?"

They agreed to meet in an hour at the diner. Hairs on his neck stood up as worry descended on him. Would she be safe for just another hour? Would it take long to get a hold of this guy? He had pulled up a photo; the guy in the diner was definitely Tony. The guy he was with was a guy named Joe Pellon. He had a rap sheet a mile long, mostly drugs and breaking and entering. Definitely someone had pulled some strings to keep this guy on the street. There was more to this story. Jayden didn't want to wait an hour.

Jayden closed down the computer and raced over to Chloe's apartment. The door was still locked so he used the spare key and went in. Nothing looked disturbed from last night. There were no traces of Chloe and he knew that she had purposely left it that way. The back door caught his eye as he went into the kitchen. It was shut, but the dead bolt was off. He had locked it himself last night.

Damn, someone had been there. Knowing no traces of Chloe were left, he felt a bit more at ease, but still anxiety filled him.

* * *

Chloe opened her eyes slowly. She hadn't slept so soundly in quite a while. She looked around at the unfamiliar light. The light blue walls were clean, decorated with a few landscape photos. Sun streamed in from the lone window across the room.

Last night, she had told Jayden everything, except about the baby. She was afraid to mention it. She had the hope that there could be more, but fear of Jayden walking away when he knew of the pregnancy filled her. Carla had assured her she wouldn't bring it up.

Her stomach grumbled. She swung her legs out of bed and sat up slowly. She stood and started taking clothes out of her bag. She didn't know how long she would be staying here, but wanted to give Jayden a chance to at least run a background check on Tony before taking off. If he didn't find something soon, she would be leaving and finding a new place to hide. The thought of it left her with an ache in her chest.

Dressed and having used the bathroom, Chloe started down the stairs. She froze as a man's voice filtered up the stairs. No one she recognized, but fear gripped her. Had one of Tony's men found her? Sarah didn't sound upset and in fact she was quite friendly with him.

Chloe continued down the stairs and hesitated a moment before she started to the kitchen, hoping to not be noticed.

"Chloe, can you come here for a second?" Sarah called.

She hesitantly turned and walked into the living room to see an elderly gentleman sitting on the couch. Sarah stood from the chair and motioned for Chloe to sit.

"This is Dr. Eldridge. I asked him to stop by because Carla mentioned your condition. I thought we should have you checked out. You certainly don't have to, but it might give you a sense of security knowing your baby is healthy and how soon you should be checked again." Sarah spoke quietly and directly, but with enough concern in her voice that Chloe had to admire her initiative.

"That's fine. As far as I can tell I'm about four months along."

"Chloe, if it's alright with you, I would like to listen to the heartbeat and do an internal exam. It'll give me a better idea how far along you are. If there are any questions, I have a portable ultrasound machine," Dr. Eldridge said. "I know you don't know me but Sarah will be right with you the whole time. I come here regularly to do checkups on the women or if someone is sick. I won't let anyone know you are here."

Chloe stiffened at the words. She needed to have her pregnancy monitored, but she was scared someone had followed him. Tony had so many doctors and other professionals in his back pocket she didn't know who to trust.

"Sarah, can I speak with you in the kitchen for a moment?" Chloe stood. "If you don't mind, Doctor?"

"Not at all." He sat back.

Chloe and Sarah went into the kitchen where they were alone. Chloe paced around the small room before saying anything.

"Chloe, I know this scares you. I've been there. You don't know who to trust. And seeing a man here when you first wake up is probably a shock." Sarah took a breath and studied Chloe for her reaction

"I didn't know Carla told you that I was pregnant."

Sarah was slow to answer. "She had your best interest in mind. Jayden still doesn't know. We both agreed that would be your place to tell him when you're ready. Carla and I both have been pregnant and in an abusive relationship. We understand the misgivings you have on trusting anyone, and we both are honored that you have trusted us."

Chloe stopped pacing and stared at her toes. She knew the right thing to do was to have the exam. "Okay, I'll do it," she whispered. "I don't want Jayden to know though."

"Your secret is safe. It will be just Carla, myself, and Dr. Eldridge who know."

With her thoughts racing, Chloe held Sarah's hand through the exam. The doctor confirmed she was a little over four months along and offered the ultrasound if she wanted to know the sex. Chloe refused at this time. He left her with a bottle of prenatal vitamins and instructions on what to look for in the way of complications, but felt she was healthy and should have no problems. He reiterated the need for milk and protein rich foods to keep her strength up, reminding her she needed to gain a bit of weight for the baby to be healthy. He promised he would check in with her in a month if she was still there. If not, he recommended she seek a check-up monthly until she was closer to her due date.

Once the doctor left, Chloe shut herself in her room. She sat on the bed and let go of the tears that had been threatening to flow. They coursed down her cheeks at the losses she had gone through. Her parents, her home, the thought of love in her life. She was thrilled with the baby coming, but now longed for Jayden to be a part of her life. How could that happen? Would he ever forgive her for not telling him, and if he did, would he want her and another man's child?

A quiet knock on the door brought Chloe back from the indulgence of self-pity she had allowed herself to wallow in. "Come in."

Carla poked her head in. "You want some company?"

Chloe stood as Carla came in. She threw her arms around her friend and Carla hugged her tight.

"You doing okay?" Carla sat beside Chloe.

"Yes. A doctor came by and confirmed I'm four months along." Chloe picked at a thread on the quilt. "I didn't know you had told Sarah."

"I wanted to be sure you were okay. I don't know what your plans are, but at least it's a start for now." Carla grabbed her hand. "Chloe, Jayden is concerned for you. Don't you want to share everything with him?"

"NO." Chloe jumped from the forcefulness of the word that escaped. "I mean, I don't know what to say to him."

"His feelings aren't going to change for you."

Chloe looked at her friend. "His feelings?"

"You know what I'm talking about. You know he has feelings for you. Just look at the way he looks at you and wants to protect you. That's more than just being a police officer, Chloe." Carla paused. "I think you feel the same for him."

"I'm not in a position to have feelings for anyone right now. Look at me. My life is a wreck. I'm carrying another man's child. What man wants to get messed up with that?"

"I think you're underestimating him, but you need to do what you're comfortable with. He wants to stop by later and see you."

Chloe shook her head. "I think it would be best if he stayed away. Honestly, Carla, I don't know what to say to him."

"If you change your mind, Sarah knows how to reach me and I can get a hold of him. Don't shut others out. Arden is your home now."

After Carla had left, Chloe stood looking out the window. The street below was empty. She pondered her friend's words about Jayden. Did he really have feelings for her? She knew she was falling for him, but she didn't know him very well. There were still so many secrets on her end and she really knew nothing about his past. If nothing else, her relationship with Tony had taught her she couldn't trust anyone and she needed to know more about him. Everyone had skeletons in their closet.

CHAPTER THIRTEEN

Jayden waited at the counter for his PI friend, David. They had been great friends when Jayden worked in Portland. David had checked on him for months after the shooting. David had tried getting Jayden into counseling beyond what was required from the department, but he refused thinking he could forget the incident. And he had until this guy showed up looking for Chloe.

Carla broke through his thoughts. "She doesn't want to see you."

Jayden clenched his hands. "Why not? Why push me away?"

"She's in shock that Tony found her. She feels she let her guard down. Give her some time."

Jayden shook his head. "I don't want to give her time. I want to protect her."

Carla squeezed his hand. "If you really care about her, let her be for now."

Jayden stilled at Carla's words. How much did he care for her? Was this love he was falling into?

As the door opened. David walked in. He pointed to a booth in the back and they made their way there. Carla had already prepared hamburgers and fries for them and brought them out, leaving them alone. She knew Jayden was getting information, but also knew Jayden would tell her as much as he could.

"Whatcha got?" Jayden said as soon as the food was placed in front of them.

"I can't even get a bite in?" David joked as he picked up a fry.

"I don't know how much time we have."

"Okay. Anthony Massey is one mean dude. You can't find any information on him because his real name is Anthony Petroni. He is bad news. A rap sheet a mile long involving possession and selling drugs. There has been talk about a few disappearances of people in association with his name, but then he fell off the grid and no one could find him. We're looking at a mafia wannabe." David picked up his burger and took a huge bite.

Jayden watched him. "That's it?"

"What do you mean 'that's it'? Man, you have no idea what I just told you. This guy has connections somewhere. No outstanding warrants, but he's a dangerous man. He's careful about staying under the radar though." David took another bite as Jayden glared at him.. "How involved are you with the girl?"

"What? I'm not involved." Jayden pushed the fries around on his plate with his fork.

"Man, you've got it bad." His friend chuckled. "I don't think I've ever seen you like this."

Jayden scowled at him. "I don't know what I feel."

"Yeah, but not like any Joe off the street. You want to protect the one you think you're falling in love with."

Jayden pushed his plate away. There was no use denying it. The question became, what do I do about it?

Carla came over to pick up the plates. She raised an eyebrow at Jayden and he just shook his head. "Chief, there is some word that a couple of guys were checking out the alley behind the diner this afternoon while I was gone. Want to take a guess at who they must be?"

"Where did you hear that?" Jayden sat up.

"The Brantley twins stopped in for sodas and they were talking about it. Their description matched those two from earlier. How are you going to find them?"

Jayden gestured for her to sit with them. "I didn't tell you yet, but Chloe's apartment was broken into after we left."

"I knew there was someone there last night. I felt them watching when we left."

"Nothing was touched, but the dead bolt was off the kitchen door and I personally locked it myself. I don't want Chloe to know this."

Carla looked at him. "I'm not staying away from my own house so don't even think of it."

"I had a feeling you would say that." Jayden glanced at David. "That's why I thought David could stay with you for a few days."

Carla stood and picked up the plates. "Clever. That's fine, but just so you know, Jayden, you are not changing my routine. And don't be so slow to tell her how you feel before she slips away."

Jayden watched Carla walk into the kitchen. Did everyone know how he felt about Chloe?

According to David, Joe was Tony's right hand man, but with Tony's background he wouldn't hesitate to cut Joe loose if it meant he could get away. How bad did Tony want to find Chloe? What end would it come to? If push came to shove, he didn't know if he could draw his weapon and defend her.

"So what do we do to draw him out?" Jayden tapped his fingers against his glass.

"Well, it would be tricky. He's not on his home turf so we can't just set up a drug buy and grab him." David pondered.

"Would he know you if you two came face to face?" Jayden paused. "He knows who I am."

"It's hard to tell. If any of his guys are as good as I am at digging things up, he knows both of our backgrounds." Dave sat back. "You know you've got nothing concrete to legally help her?"

"I know, I know. It's so damn frustrating that she won't ask for help."

* * *

Chloe paced the room. She didn't want to run, but her gut instinct said she needed to get away. Her car was at the apartment and she didn't have a way to get back there. Would Carla bring it to her? If she could convince Carla she needed it just in case Tony got close then maybe she would. She picked up her cell phone and dialed Carla. When Carla's phone went to voice mail, she hung up without leaving a message. A fear nagged at her and she questioned Carla's safety. She needed to either leave and draw attention away from Arden, or she had to confront Tony. Doubt filled her. She didn't want to put her baby in danger.

She wandered around the big house and found the others in the living room and sat to listen. She didn't know how they had come to be here, or if anyone of them had transportation. She had kept to herself, stayed distant. As Chloe listened to some of their stories, their common link was Carla. At one time or another Carla had known each of them and gotten them to safety. Sarah had been here for years and never worried about being found. Her husband had divorced her on grounds of abandonment and she was okay with that. He had remarried and had stopped looking for her. Sarah became the go-between for the girls and Carla for information as she felt the safest move about the town.

"Do you all have vehicles here?" Chloe asked.

Sarah glanced around the room at the others. "No, Chloe. No one does, but me. It was easier to get rid of them. Or actually, Carla took care of them so none of us could be traced here. If you need to get somewhere Carla can take you."

Chloe sat back in shock. "None of you have a way to leave if one of your exes find you?"

"It hasn't happened in all these years. We feel it's better not to have anything tied to us here." Melissa spoke up. "Do you need to be somewhere else? I honestly am not sure there is anywhere safer than right here."

"I just didn't know how it worked." Chloe's mind raced with possibilities of leaving. The bus station was down the road. If Tony was busy in Arden she could get a ticket as far away as possible. Afterward, she could message him and draw him elsewhere, anywhere to get him away from Carla and Jayden.

As it came closer to dinner, the girls dispersed to start cooking and setting up. Sarah and Chloe remained in the living room. "Chloe, please don't think of running," Sarah spoke softly.

"Why would you think that?"

Sarah moved closer to her. "We've all been there. Our instinct is to run."

"I don't want Jayden or Carla to get hurt."

"I know you don't. Carla has taken care of herself for years and can be pretty fierce. I know you care about Jayden, but he's trained to protect. You can trust him." Sarah gave Chloe a hug.

Chloe picked up the double meaning of trusting Jayden, but her stomach tensed at the thought of trusting anyone again.

CHAPTER FOURTEEN

Darkness fell. Chloe stood in the living room behind the curtain looking out. She had been hoping Jayden would show up. She told Carla she didn't want to see him, but she had almost convinced herself that he wouldn't listen.

The street lit up as a car cruised slowly down the road. Chloe shrank back against the wall and breathed a sigh of relief when the car continued on. She prayed it hadn't been Tony. He would be brazen enough to just come to the front door.

Chloe stayed in the living room listening to the house settle around her. It was well after midnight before all the women had made their ways to their bedrooms . She sat in the dark pondering her next move. She was certain that if she moved on Jayden would be safe. She worried about Carla also, but Jayden was foremost in her mind. It would kill her if something happened to him.

Chloe crept up the stairs to collect her bag. She packed everything as quiet as she could and had just started to open the door when the downstairs door opened. Slipping into the hallway, she moved quickly to Sarah's room, opened the door and called her name.

Sarah jumped from bed. She grabbed the fireplace poker, and motioned for Chloe to move out of the way. As they stepped into the hallway, the living room light flicked on. She crept down the stairs.

"Sarah?" a voice called out. "It's me, Carla."

"What are you doing here? You scared Chloe half to death."

"I was worried she might try to run," Carla explained. "I thought I would spend the night here, but it took me longer to get here. Needed to make sure no one was following me."

"What's going on?" Chloe stood in the doorway. "Has Jayden found out anything?"

"Come on in and sit down." Carla curled her feet under her in the chair. "A PI friend of Jayden has come in from Portland to give him some help. He got some background information on Tony."

"What kind of information?"

"I don't know the details. Jayden asked David to stay at my house for a couple of days to help him." Carla was vague and hoped Chloe would let it go.

Chloe closed her eyes. "Is he okay?"

Carla smiled. "Yes, he is fine other than being upset that you don't want to see him. I have never seen him act this way over a woman before."

After some small talk, all three women headed up to bed. Carla decided to sleep on a cot in Chloe's room.

Chloe knew she was keeping an eye on her, but she seemed content to stay for the night and not run. Chloe slid into bed and laid awake, her thoughts on Jayden. Even as she finally drifted off as the sun was coming up, Jayden was in her dreams and she felt safe.

* * *

Jayden sat back in his chair and put his hands behind his head. He had been at the office all night looking for all the information he could find on Tony now that he had his real name. The drug charges had never stuck and he served no real time. The implications of missing associates of his had no evidence that Tony was involved, although everything pointed to him. The photos all came up showing a resemblance, but there were no recent pictures. He needed to arrest him in order to run his fingerprints.

He picked up his phone. He wanted so badly to call the number Carla had given him for Chloe. But he promised to only call if necessary, but his heart was telling him it was necessary. He needed to hear her voice and know she was okay. His mind argued with his heart because it knew he needed to respect her privacy right now. Carla had promised to add his cell number to Chloe's contacts so she would have it.

Betty walked in. "You've been here all night and there's no fresh coffee?" Jayden stood and stretched.

"I was working, not making coffee." Jayden moved to the coffeepot.

Betty swatted his hand away. "I'll make it. You look like hell. What's got you all fired up? I don't recall hearing about any crime sprees."

"Just something I'm helping Dave on." Jayden felt a twinge of guilt, he hated to lie. Betty could help with research, but Jayden couldn't risk telling anyone else about Chloe. "I'm going to run out. I'll be back in a bit."

Jayden slipped out the door before Betty could ask any more questions. He started for the diner to find Carla. He made a quick detour to his apartment for a shower and change of clothes. In record time he was out. As he came around the corner, he noticed a car parked near the beach. Driving slowly he made a mental note on license plate. He pulled into the diner and punched the number into the car computer. Just as he suspected Tony's name came up. At least he now knew what he drove.

He shut down the computer and walked into the diner. Carla was busy serving breakfast to the locals. Jayden knew she was missing Chloe's help, yet hadn't said a word. Some of the locals had asked about Chloe, and Carla simply said she had a personal issue that she needed to tend to. No further questions were forthcoming. He helped himself to a cup of coffee and sat at the counter.

"Usual, chief?" Carla asked as she headed to the kitchen.

"Yeah, that's fine."

With orders in and a bit of a breather, Carla refilled Jayden's cup. "Any news?"

"Our friend is sitting down the street watching the diner." Jayden was quiet in his answer. He glanced around, but everyone was chatting among themselves. "Was she okay last night?"

Carla held up her finger as she went to gather orders to deliver. She got all the food out and slid Jayden's plate in front of him. "Funny, she was more concerned about you."

Jayden paused before taking a bite. He felt Carla's eyes on him waiting for his response. "Do you think she'll stick around?"

"I don't know. Sarah said she was asking questions about cars and how the women would leave if someone ever found them." She grabbed the coffeepot and made rounds to the tables. Making her way back to the counter, she held the pot in front of Jayden. He shook his head.

"We can't let her run." Desperation filled his voice.

"She'll be fine. Give her some credit. She got this far and she has made the effort to get away from that man." She squeezed his hand. "Jocelyn just pulled in. How much does she know?"

"Nothing." He finished his breakfast in silence waiting for his sister to pounce on him. He figured she had stopped by the office and Betty told her he had worked all night.

He felt a nudge in the back. "Hey, bro. What's happening?"

Jocelyn slid onto the stool next to him. She was a beautiful woman, yet a very strong willed who seemed to scare men off. "Nothing with me. You?"

She stood there searching his face. He didn't know what she was after, but she wasn't in any hurry.

"Not much," she said. "I hear David is in town."

"Ahh, so that's what brings you to see me."

"What? It simply was a conversation starter."

"To what? Yes, he's still available. Why don't you just tell him you changed your mind and you will go out on a date with him?" David had been pursuing his sister for years, but for some unknown reason, Jocelyn, although she liked David, turned him down every time he asked her out.

"I'm not looking for a date. Just curious as to why he's here in Arden, away from the big city life."

Jayden thought carefully. "He decided to come visit an old friend."

"Hmmm, I'm not sure I believe that, but okay. " She played with the saltshaker on the counter. "Is there anything else you want to tell me?"

"Like what?" Jayden sighed. "What exactly are you fishing for, sis? I don't really have time for games this morning."

"I'm not fishing for anything. Just haven't really chatted with you since the new girl showed up in town. How's that going?"

Jayden rolled his eyes. "Give it a rest. She is just a new person in the community. There is nothing there."

The laughter that rolled out of his sister made him smile. "I would love a sister-in-law."

Jayden stood. "That's my cue to leave." He gave her a kiss on the cheek. "I love you, but stay out of my love life, or lack of one."

Her laughter followed him as he left the diner. He shook his head. She could get under his skin, but she was one of the best friends he ever had. He had never met siblings closer than him and Jocelyn. Chloe would love her when she got to know her.

CHAPTER FIFTEEN

Chloe woke with a start. Carla was gone. She lay in bed and stared at the ceiling. She had to move on. She sighed as her thoughts drifted to the kiss she had shared with Jayden. She had never felt so alive, yet the secret of her pregnancy weighed on her. The only way she saw it ending was with Jayden hating her and she would need to move on anyway. Now was just as good a time as any to go.

Chloe swung her feet over the side of the bed and sat there. She would write a good-bye letter to Carla. It was better to break it off clean with Jayden. Mind made up, she rummaged through her bag for clean clothes. Repacking after she was dressed, she sat with paper and a pen.

Chloe chewed the end of the pen as her thoughts raced on what to say to Carla. Everything seemed too trite. Frustrated, she pushed the paper aside and threw down the pen. She would just go and make a clean break from both of them. She had Carla's number if she chose to call later. The question was how to get out of the house without being seen. The bus station was down the street, but walking there with her suitcase would look a bit obvious.

As she started downstairs, she heard murmuring in the living room. She paused and strained her ears to make out the conversation. Not being able to, she continued. Upon entering the living room, Sarah paused her talking to Michelle.

"I didn't mean to interrupt." Chloe hesitated.

"You didn't. Come in." Sarah smiled at Michelle.

Michelle stood. "I've got kitchen clean-up so I best get started."

Chloe stepped aside as she left the room. She tugged at her shirt and sat on the edge of the couch. "What's going on?"

"Nothing." There were no other words forthcoming and the silence was deafening. Chloe sat rigid. Her mind raced with the possibilities. Had Tony found her? Was Carla hurt? Where was Jayden?

"Chloe?" Sarah's soft voice broke through her thoughts.

"Yes?"

"I know what you're thinking. You are safe here. Jayden is doing everything he can to catch up with Tony and put him behind bars."

Chloe sighed. "I can't explain it. I just don't want anyone in danger."

"There's nothing to explain. We've all been there." Sarah leaned back in her chair. "Did I ever tell you my story?"

"No."

"I was a teen when I got involved with Jimmy. I thought I was so in love. Things were good for a while and he treated me right."

"What happened?" Chloe pushed back onto the couch and waited.

"Well, I got pregnant and Jimmy didn't want a baby. We had just gotten married and he thought I got pregnant on purpose. His anger escalated from there. I couldn't say anything that appeased him."

Sarah stood and walked to the window. She pushed back the curtain and stared outside. Finally when she turned back around, tears were streaming. "He pushed me and I fell down the stairs. I lost the baby. It was at that moment I knew I had to get out. Chloe, we've all been there, scared, afraid to ask for help, determined to run even when we were being helped. Don't you see you're not alone in this?"

"You don't know Tony."

"You're right, I don't, but I know his type. If you run and he finds you, when Jayden isn't around to help, and if you survive it, your baby might not. Is that what you want?"

Chloe stood. Her hands clenched at her sides. "Of course not. I left him so I could protect my baby. Do you think I would deliberately put myself in harm's way?"

"No, not deliberately. But I do think you could put yourself in harm's way by not thinking."

Chloe struggled to hold back the tears. "You don't understand." She turned and ran. As she stumbled up the stairs, the tears started flowing like a sieve. Slamming the bedroom door, she threw herself on the bed and let the sobs take over.

As the tears subsided, Chloe fell into a restless sleep, dreaming of running from Tony. *She was stuck in the room, cut off from the door. Tony smirked at her and advanced one painfully slow step at a time. The anxiety of what would be coming when he reached her had Chloe gasping for air. His right hand slammed into the wall beside her head while his left hand rested just to the other side of her, pinning her to the wall. No escape. Panic filled her and the air seemed to be cut off as she tried to take in deep breaths. His fingers traced along her jaw line until they were encircled around her neck.*

She woke with a start chocking on her fear, her hands rubbing her neck as the feeling of being choked slowly dissipated. Her head pounded with the start of a migraine from exhaustion that had racked her body. Chloe curled up, pulling her knees tight to her chest and for the first time in a long time wished she knew how to pray.

* * *

Jayden drove by the apartment where Chloe had stayed. He pulled into a space behind her car. Sitting there just staring at the building, he felt the dull ache of loneliness in his chest. He had loved the conversations they had, the shyness about her. Loved? Where did that come from? He sighed as he put the car in Drive. He had to see her. He had to know she was alright.

The driving need propelled the car in the direction of

the women's shelter, keeping a close watch on the rearview mirror. Satisfied he wasn't being followed, he moved his head from side to side to ease the tension. Only when the house came into sight did he feel a relief, and a burning desire to hold her in his arms. He needed to assure her things would be okay.

Sarah met him at the door. "I'm not sure it's a good idea for you to be here, Jayden."

"Why not? I just want to talk to her."

"She's struggling to know she's safe." Sarah sat at the kitchen table and gestured for Jayden to take one of the other chairs.

"You think if she sees me she won't feel safe?"

Sarah pondered the question. "I think in her mind you are in grave danger and that you can lead Tony here to her."

"That's ridiculous. Let me see her, Sarah." His intense stare held her eyes.

She sighed and stood. "I'll see if she wants to. If she doesn't, you need to respect that."

"Fine."

Jayden stood and paced around the kitchen. Was Chloe really feeling unsafe with him? The thought of it was unfathomable to him.

"Hey." Chloe's soft voice behind him caused him to pause before turning.

"Are you okay?" He took a few steps towards her and stopped.

"I'm doing okay." Chloe trembled. His arms ached to hold her, yet she moved towards the table and sat down.

Jayden followed her lead and sat beside her. "Did you know Tony went by an alias?"

"Alias?"

"Tony's real last name is Petroni. He's involved in dealing drugs, for sure, but there is question about some other things he may be involved in."

Chloe's eyes widened. "I had no idea. I knew he was doing something illegal, but he never talked about it so I didn't know any details. I had overhead some things, vague things, but nothing specific."

"I'm not judging you. I want to help, but Chloe you have to tell me everything."

She stood up. "I have told you everything." Her voice trembled. She bit her bottom lip as she met his eyes. "I don't want you to be hurt, Jayden. I-I don't have anything else to tell you."

Jayden searched her face. Something was off, but he couldn't put a finger on it. "Chloe." He took a step towards her and reached out a hand.

"Don't, please." Chloe stepped back. "I can't Jayden. Please you'll be better off if you don't come back here." She turned and fled from the room.

Jayden was numb, he ached to hold her. To make her believe she could trust him. But the alarming voice in his head kept whispering that something was still wrong. How could he protect her if she shut him out? He ran his hand over his face. He was tired and losing perspective. He needed some rest to clear his mind.

He turned, left the house, not looking back. He wouldn't push her, but he would get her justice.

CHAPTER SIXTEEN

Tony stood across the street from the diner. Carla was just turning the Open sign around. Now was the perfect time to get some answers before anyone came in. He crossed the street and chose a seat at the counter.

"What can I get you?" Carla's voice was cool, but polite.

"Coffee, please." Tony's eyes stayed on her as she filled his cup.

"Anything else?"

"Just some answers." He sat back and took a sip of the hot beverage.

"I can't imagine what I could possibly answer for you. You need directions?"

"I want to know where Chloe is." He sat forward and watched her instinctively step back. He smiled.

"I don't know what you're talking about. There is no Chloe here."

Tony chuckled. "Obviously she is not here, but don't play coy. I know you know where she is."

"I have no answers for you. If you don't want the coffee, there's the door. If you're going to stay, drink it and be quiet." She turned her back to him and headed to the kitchen.

Tony finished his coffee in the time she was gone. It was just a matter of minutes before the chief showed up. He was sure she had called him. The door opened behind him. A couple of elderly men walked in and chose a seat. They were involved in their own conversation and oblivious to him.

Carla came from the kitchen. With a quick look at Tony, she put on a smile and greeted the other customers. Spending a few minutes in quiet small talk, she took their order.

"Refill, please," Tony called out as she headed to the kitchen.

Walking to the counter, she stood watching him for a brief moment. "Sorry, we're out. That cup's on the house."

He snickered. "Trying to get rid of me?"

The door opened and the chair next to him was filled. He glanced over to see the Chief of Police. "Chief."

"I think you're done here, unless you want answers from me?" Jayden gestured for coffee. "Of course, I would expect answers from you first."

Tony threw down a couple of dollars on the counter. "Thanks for the coffee, and the enlightening information, Carla."

* * *

Jayden raised an eyebrow at Carla who shook her head ever so slightly. As soon as the door shut behind him, she threw her towel on the counter. "I told him nothing. What information?"

"He's just yanking your chain. Ignore him." Jayden pushed his coffee aside. "David's trailing him. Thankfully, from the questions he is asking, he has no idea where Chloe is."

"Did you talk to her?"

Jayden sighed. "Yeah, a bit. She doesn't want me there and wants me to not contact her. What's the deal with her? It's more than Tony."

Carla played with the towel. "Only she knows if there is."

Jayden shook his head and stood. "Carla, I love you, but you have to stop protecting her."

"Me? Jayden, you want to protect her just as much as I do. But until you can admit your true feelings for her, to her, you need to stop acting like you can save her. Give everyone a break and get things straightened out between you. You can't look at things objectively if you're lying to yourself."

"I'm not lying to myself." Jayden jerked his hat off the counter. "We have a connection, but beyond that, I don't know."

"You keep telling yourself that." Carla picked up the towel and turned towards the kitchen as Jayden left. He was ticked for her pushing him, but he was going to lose Chloe if he didn't start being honest. The big concern right now was keeping Tony from finding her. Carla knew firsthand the danger if he did.

CHAPTER SEVENTEEN

Tony grimaced as he shifted in his seat. His legs cramped and he was getting sick and tired of watching the diner. He needed to find Chloe. He was tired of putting up with the run-around from Carla, and her cop friend. His gut told him they both knew where she was.

He straightened up as Carla locked the building and started towards her house. She usually went home and stayed there, however he saw her, and Jayden, in a heated exchanged. *This was it.* Tonight could be the night she led him right to Chloe.

He waited for her to round the corner then he drove down the block, circling around. She crossed to the other side of the street and was almost to her house. He slowed as he drove past., but she never looked up. She was staring at the sidewalk, obviously deep in thought. He pulled up to the corner and waited. His anxiety grew as time ticked on and he reached for the Tums to calm the heartburn.

Tony's cell phone vibrated against his hip. Grabbing it, he glanced at the caller ID. "You best have good news."

The silence that greeted him gave him the answer. "Sorry, boss. Still nothing."

"Don't bother checking in if you can't find her." Tony paused. "The PI is yours. Get him out of the picture." He hung up. Watching through the rearview mirror, Carla entered her house. Lights came on as she moved about the house. He sighed. How much longer would this go on? Chloe could not have just fallen off the face of the earth with her car still here.

A knock on the window startled Tony. He came face to face with the Chief of Police. He cracked the window. "Something I can do for you, officer?"

"Sure. You can move along. There's no reason for you to be sitting here."

Tony shrugged his shoulders. "Fine." He started the car as Jayden took a step back and stood there. He gunned it and took off, curses filling the vehicle as he rounded the corner.

* * *

Jayden snickered as he started down the road towards Carla's. They knew Tony had been trailing her. She called him as soon as she stepped foot in her house. Jayden shook his head. He would have loved to have seen her squeeze through the fence to get to her car. He expected her call as soon as she talked with Chloe.

Jayden went through her house, shutting off lights and locking up once more. He turned and headed to the police station. Tony was in for a shock when he circled back around like he had numerous nights now.

At the station, Jayden filled his mug and shut himself in his office. He paced and sipped his coffee. He needed to know Chloe was okay. He couldn't bear the thought of anything happening to her. Everyone said his feelings were obvious. If so, then why was he struggling to sort them out in his head? He sighed as he sank into the chair. He couldn't imagine his life alone. Suddenly Chloe filled his every thought, awake or asleep.

The ringing phone startled Jayden. "Peterson here."

"Jayden, Chloe's gone." The panic in Carla's voice made Jayden sit up straight.

"What do you mean she's gone? Where?" He slammed his fist on his desk top.

"I don't know. The girls didn't know anything. She said she had a headache and went up to bed before dinner. When Sarah checked on her a couple of hours later, she was gone."

Jayden clenched his jaw tight. Tony didn't have her, she ran. He ran his fingers through his hair and gripped a handful as his mind reeled with thoughts of where she could have gone. How is he supposed to protect her if she's not at the safe house?

"I'm on my way." Jayden slammed the phone back on the receiver before Carla had a chance to respond. He sent a quick to text to David letting him know to keep a close eye on Tony.

The drive to the women's shelter took forever. Jayden's mind raced with every possibility that could have caused Chloe to run. There was more going on. His heart ached at the thought of never seeing her again.

He turned into the driveway in the back of the house and entered through the kitchen. Carla jumped up from the table. He pulled her close. "We'll find her," he whispered. He didn't know how, but he would.

"Did you go to the bus station and see if she had been there?"

Carla looked up at him. "Yes, but they weren't very helpful. Maybe seeing your uniform will help jog their memory."

"Maybe. I'll go over there now and see." Jayden looked over at Sarah. "Anything missing in the house that would give us a clue where she went?"

Sarah shook her head. "Nothing's missing that I know of."

"I'll be back." Jayden turned toward the door and stopped. "Carla, we'll catch up with her."

She nodded. He felt her eyes on him as he left. He couldn't lose Chloe.

He consciously cleared his mind as he entered the bus station. The young man behind the counter looked up uninterested. "Help you?"

"I hope so. I'm looking for someone. Young woman, thin, blonde hair probably pulled back in a ponytail."

"Doesn't ring a bell." The clerk stared at Jayden. "Anything else?"

"Look, this is important. This girl is in trouble and I need to find her. Are you sure you haven't sold any tickets in the past few hours to a young, single woman?"

"Maybe. I can't remember everyone that comes in here." The young man shrugged.

"You can't possibly sell that many tickets that you can't remember." Jayden slammed his hand on the sill of the ticket window. "Think!"

"Okay, okay. I sold a few tickets today. There was one young girl, had a baseball cap on. She bought a one-way ticket to Portland. Bus left five minutes ago."

"Thanks."

Jayden turned toward the door and pulled out his cell phone. Punching in David's number he walked to his car.

"She's got a ticket to Portland." Jayden's voice trembled on the last word.

"You want me to go?" Jayden knew his friend wanted to make sure he was ready. David understood what going back to Portland would cost him.

"Keep an eye on Tony."

"He's not going anywhere. He doesn't have a clue." Dave paused. "You sure you want to go yourself?"

"Yeah. I need to do this. I just don't know where to start."

David chuckled. "How about the bus station?"

"Wise guy. Take care of Carla while I'm gone. I'll contact the station and get someone to fill in for me." Jayden hung up. His hand shook as he pocketed his phone. Portland. God, how could he go there?

CHAPTER EIGHTEEN

Although Portland was only an hour and half away, the drive dragged on. He didn't know how much of a head start Chloe had. He had to find her before Tony figured she was gone from Arden.

He pulled into the Portland Bus Station, cut the engine, got out of his car and sprinted inside. Glancing around, he made his way to the counter.

"Has the bus from Arden arrived yet?"

The clerk glanced at his computer. "Looks like it got in about five minutes ago. Last slot to your left."

"Thanks." Jayden rushed thought the station then turned the corner and stopped. Chloe was standing there with her bag on her feet, just looking around. His heart raced. The brokenness she portrayed felt like a sucker-punch to his gut. He just wanted to pull her into his arms and never let her go.

He took a deep breath and stepped forward. As he closed the space between them, he never took his eyes off her. She was unaware of him and he was struck by how vulnerable she was if Tony had been the one to find her.

"Chloe." His voice was low as he came around to the front of her.

She looked at him in horror. "How did you find me?"

Jayden searched her face. This was a delicate situation. He didn't want to frighten her. "Really?" He joked. "I'm a cop."

Tears filled her eyes. "Please, Jayden. Forget you saw me."

"Chloe, I can't." He reached for her hand. She didn't fight him when he took it in his. "I'm worried. Tony is looking for you. Why did you leave the house?"

"He'll find me. I have to move on." She closed her eyes, but a tear broke broke through and slipped down her cheek.. "You don't understand."

Jayden pulled her close and wrapped his arms around her. He felt her soften and her arms wrap around his waist. "Let me help you. Chloe, I can't bear the thought of anything happening to you." He kissed the top of her head. "Talk to me."

Chloe looked up at him. Her eyes were red from holding back tears. "There's so much you don't know."

"So tell me. I'm not going anywhere."

Chloe looked around. "Not here."

"Let me take you back to the shelter." Jayden picked up her bag.

"No!" Chloe took a ridge stance. "I won't go back there and put everyone in danger."

Jayden sighed. "He can't find you there."

"Jayden, he will find me. I won't be responsible for anything happening to the others. Please."

Jayden's heart sank. She was scared. His stomach clenched in apprehension. If push came to shove, would he lose Chloe because of his inabilities?

"Okay. Let's go to my apartment for now and talk." He took a few steps. "Okay?"

She nodded. As they made their way to Jayden's car, they were silent. Jayden felt her tenseness as they walked side by side. He wanted nothing more than to hold her again as she slid past him into the front seat.

He placed her bag on the backseat before he came around and slid into the driver's seat. He started the car. "You ready?"

"Yes." The word was barely audible. Her eyes never left her clenched hands in her lap.

Jayden sighed. God help him. His silent prayer shocked him. Where would this lead?

CHAPTER NINETEEN

Jayden drove back to Arden in silence. The steady breathing from Chloe let him know she was sleeping. She must be exhausted. In a glance, he took her in head to toe. Her arms wrapped around her midsection, yet she appeared relaxed.

He sighed. And what was he thinking bringing her to his house? He shook his head. He had to get the truth out of her and find out exactly what had happened between her and Tony. Jayden adjusted the radio so the music could be heard softly. The classic rock station soothed his nerves as he drummed his fingers on the steering wheel in time with the beat.

He pulled into his driveway and turned off the car. The street was quiet as it normally was at this time of night. He checked the clock. Midnight. Turning in his seat, he just watched her sleep. Her features were softened and her hair fell gently over one eye. He reached out and brushed it back, his fingers lingering. He smiled as her eyes fluttered open and she met his .

"Are we here?"

Jayden nodded, not wanting to speak, but to just hold on to this moment.

"Should we go in?" Chloe sat up, breaking contact.

"Yes, I guess so." Jayden opened the door and stepped out. Taking a deep breath of the night air, he went around the car and opened her door. Extending his hand to help her out of the car, there was the slightest hesitation on Chloe's part before she took his hand. He pulled her upright and looked down at her. Her eyes were wide, but met his. He longed to reach down and kiss her lips. He wanted to feel her against him, her warmth to envelop him.

He cleared his throat and stepped aside. He reached for her bag as she shut the car door. Jayden gestured towards the house, his hand on the small of her back as they walked toward the door. Being so close to her, and yet having to show restraint made time move in slow motion. He took in the empty street, satisfied that Tony was not around.

"Feel free to get some sleep. We can talk in the morning." Jayden lingered for a moment, hoping for something from her, but not knowing what.

"Thanks." Chloe touched his arm. "I really do mean it. I don't know what I would do without you."

With a small smile, Jayden nodded toward the living room. It was going to be a long night. He settled into the recliner and tried to think of a way to break through Chloe's defenses. She was strong, but determined to not let anyone in. A deadly combination as far as he was concerned. He couldn't risk falling in love with her. *Love? Where did that come from?* He closed his eyes and, as he drifted off to sleep, memories of his life in Portland assaulted him. The shooting, the investigation, and his running home to Arden to get away from it all.

After dozing for an hour or so with nightmares plaguing him, Jayden awoke in a sweat. He sat up and looked around. Reality flooded back. Although the middle of the night, he grabbed his laptop and fired it up. He needed more information on Tony; he was a dangerous man and wouldn't stop until he had Chloe. Something Jayden couldn't bear to think about, He fired off an email to David, hoping he was up and online.

Within minutes, a reply came. They made arrangements for David to come over. Jayden started coffee and paced the living room while he waited. He needed a plan before Chloe woke. He could just picture her throwing a wrench into any plan he came up with. He smiled and wondered how, and when she had started consuming his every thought. He sighed. He needed to deal with his feelings and talk with her about it, but it would have to wait until after Tony was behind bars.

The soft knock at the door announced David's arrival. It was time to get down to brass tacks and find the vulnerability in Tony. Jayden didn't believe Tony really cared for Chloe. He couldn't believe it. And he certainly didn't believe Chloe had any warm feelings towards the man. She wouldn't be running if she did.

Sitting with David until the early morning, a plan formed. Jayden sat back and smiled. They could pull it off if Chloe would just cooperate.

The sun filtered slowly through the window as morning broke. Jayden got up to make fresh coffee while David slipped out. Jayden listened at Chloe's door, hearing nothing he decided to jump in the shower before she awoke. With the hot water cascading over him, he allowed himself for the moment to picture his future with Chloe. He could see it, taste it, and for once in his life, he didn't want anything more. He shut the water off, toweled off and dressed quickly.

Heading to the kitchen for coffee, he stopped short to see Chloe sitting on the couch.

"Morning."

"Morning. Did you sleep well?" Jayden sat in the recliner.

"Yes. I was out before my head hit the pillow, I think." She pulled her legs up under her. "And you? Did you sleep at all?"

Jayden shifted. "No. David stopped by." Chloe stiffened and moved back, further away from him.

"So you decided you were going to have a plan in place this morning without talking to me?"

"Why are you so against getting help?" Jayden stood and paced to the window. "Or is it just me you don't want help from?"

CHAPTER TWENTY

Chloe squeezed her eyes shut. She didn't want to see the vulnerability in Jayden's face. . She wanted to hold on to him and forget all her problems. Tell him everything, and let go of her fear and insecurities.

"It's not you. It's just something I have to do on my own." Her tiredness came through in her voice.

"Chloe." The word was just above a whisper. She heard the anguish in the simplicity of his speaking her name.

The tears rolled down her cheeks. "Jayden, I just can't." She buried her face in her hands and sobbed quietly. She felt his hands on her shoulders as he knelt in front of her. His fingers gently kneaded the tension from her.

He urged her forward until her face was buried into his shoulder and he tightened his arms around her. "Just cry and let it out. You have held it together for way too long." His voice was soft and soothing and Chloe found herself melting into him. She wrapped her arms around him and hung on tight. The sobs subsided and yet she couldn't let go.

Jayden slid his arm under her legs and carried her to the couch. He sat, pulling her onto his lap. She sighed and settled her head more against his shoulder and closed her eyes. She finally felt safe.

Jayden slowly ran his fingers up and down her arm. Her breathing slowed and her body relaxed against him. He kissed her gently on the forehead and whispered, "Let me love you."

* * *

Jayden squinted against the bright sun light that shone through the window. They had slept through the night. Chloe, still in his lap, a small smile on her lips. He wondered how she could have gotten mixed up with someone like Tony. He smiled as her eyes opened, meeting his. She blinked and sighed.

"I'm sorry." She sat up.

"Don't be. You needed a good cry, and a good night's sleep. Apparently you got both." Jayden allowed her to stand. He watched her for a brief second before standing himself. "I'll put some coffee on."

She nodded, but didn't look at him. He shook his head and started for the kitchen. He had no idea how to break through her defenses, but he had to find a way to protect her before he lost her for good.

* * *

Chloe walked into the kitchen to find Jayden staring out the window. Coffee was brewing. She stood in the doorway, unsure of what to say. How could she tell him how much she needed him to hold her every night? She needed to tell him about the baby, but the words stuck in her throat. He would never understand her running with no plan while she was pregnant. He came from a home where both parents were involved. It was unimaginable to her that her child would not have a father, but it was her fear that drove her away to protect her unborn child.

"How are you feeling? Hungry?" Jayden turned slowly to face her. His face was unreadable.

"A little." She said in a meek voice.

"How about some eggs?" He opened the refrigerator, but waited for her to answer before reaching in.

"That sounds good." She took a couple of steps into the room. "Can I help?"

"Not with cooking, but you can help by telling me what is going on." He had his back to her once more and she sighed. He was infuriating.

"Why can't you let it go, Jayden?"

"Because I want to help. When did that become such a bad thing?"

"It's not. It's just... There is so much you don't know."

Jayden glanced over his shoulder at her. She was wringing her hands together as the fear of her secret rushed through her.

"That's the point of me asking, isn't it? That I don't know."

"Where are your coffee mugs?" She fumbled with the cupboard door and poured the coffee, handing a mug to Jayden.

He grabbed the cup with one hand; his other reached for her waist. He bent forward and placed a soft kiss on her lips. "Thanks."

Her hand rested on his chest and she could feel his heart. With a soft sigh, she leaned into him and returned the kiss. The softness of his lips had her wanting more. He ran his tongue over her bottom lip. Trembling she pulled back. "Jayden?"

"It's okay. It's a kiss, Chloe. Nothing more right now."

She watched him. Taking a deep breath, she stepped back and reached for her coffee.

"Eggs are ready." Jayden slid the eggs on a plate and carried them to the table. He was amused at the way she dug into her food and was done in seconds. "Still hungry?"

"No. It was good. I know, I tend to inhale."

"You should try tasting then once in a while, you might enjoy them more." He chuckled as he ate slowly, watching her sip her coffee. She was relaxed this morning a bit, but still had her guard up.

"I didn't mean to get involved with Tony." Chloe spoke suddenly. Her eyes stayed on her cup.

Jayden pushed his plate aside. He sat back and waited for more.

"I had just lost my parents. I felt so alone. He was good to me at the beginning. And then he would lose his temper. It started as just yelling, and throwing stuff, then he got more physical as time went on." Her voice was low. She took another sip of coffee.

"I'm glad you saved yourself."

She glanced up at him. "Yes, myself." She spoke more to herself.

"So why are you not letting me help you?"

"I just feel like I have never stood on my own. It's time to do that."

"From where I'm sitting you have been on your own. There's nothing wrong with taking some help, especially in a volatile situation like this one."

"Maybe."

Jayden leaned forward and reached for her hand. "Chloe, let me in."

He was desperate to protect her and she could hear the pleading in his voice..

"It's not that simple."

"It is if you would just be truthful."

Chloe stood and took her dishes to the sink. "You think I'm not being truthful?"

"I think you're holding back. Tell me I'm wrong."

Chloe ran the water and started washing the dishes. She shook her head. "I'm not going to tell you you're wrong, all I can say is what I have said is enough."

Jayden reached past her and shut off the water. "Enough for who, Chloe? Not for me. Not when I feel you're hiding something that could end up putting your life in more danger. Not when I want to be a part of your life. I'm falling in love with you. Don't shut me out."

She faced him. "You don't want to be a part of my life, Jayden. Trouble seems to follow me wherever I go."

She felt numb inside as he backed up, heading for the deck. Once he shut the door a frustrated growl echoed from outside.

CHAPTER TWENTY-ONE

Jayden sat out on his deck, eyes closed. Since he had found out about the trouble with Chloe the nightmares had returned. Last night he had slept without them, but this morning they were on his mind. The shooting, the unnecessary dying, the investigation, and how he was ready to give up his badge. Could he even protect her if he wanted to? He had moved back to Arden to get away from the high crime, away from having to be prepared to draw his weapon. Could he even do it?

Jayden ran his fingers through his hair, trying to forget that night, the young boy that had died in his arms. He shook his head trying to clear the memories. What he needed most of all, and missed, was his dad to talk to. Dad would have had the right advice for him. Maybe his mom, or sister, could talk with Chloe.

He sat forward, elbows on his knees. Jocelyn might know what to say to her. Carla hadn't made any headway with her. With resolve, he stood. He needed to get in touch with his sister and hope Chloe wouldn't be offended.

When he stepped back inside the house, the dishes were done and kitchen was spotless. He moved into the living room, but Chloe wasn't there either. He started down the hall and heard the shower running. He breathed a sigh of relief.

He reached for his cell phone and started back to the living room. Punching in his sister's number, he sank into the couch.

"This better be good, I was still sleeping." Jocelyn's voice brought a smile to his face.

"It is. Get up and get over to my place. Need your help."

"What's up?"

"Can't talk now. Just get over here as quickly as you can." He hung up before she could respond. He didn't want to get into a long discussion on the phone and run the risk that Chloe would hear him and take off before Jocelyn got there.

* * *

Chloe straightened the bathroom. Her mind had been spinning the whole time in the shower. She needed to tell him the truth. But he said he was falling in love…the fear of those feelings changing when he found out the truth kept her from saying anything.

She wondered if she was falling in love too. What was love? Her heart pounding every time she saw him, wanting to be with him all the time, wanting the safety of his arms at night. Or was that just the fear talking, and her wanting to just jump from one bad situation to another simply because she was afraid to be alone.

She found Jayden on the couch, eyes were closed and breathing steady. She sat in the armchair and watched him snoring softly, one arm over his head. Chloe had never seen a man with such long eyelashes. It just heightened his good looks. She wanted nothing more than to go lay with him on the couch and feel his arms cocoon her from worries.

She startled out of her thoughts when the front door opened. "Jayden?"

Before Chloe could respond Jocelyn walked into the living room. "Hi, Chloe."

"Hi. He was sleeping." Chloe turned to Jayden to find his eyes on her. "I wasn't going to wake you."

Jayden sat up. "It's okay. I didn't realize I had fallen asleep. Was just waiting for you to get out of the shower." He stood and pulled his sister into a bear hug. "Maybe you can visit with Chloe while I make a couple of phone calls."

"Sure." Jocelyn gave him a puzzled look, but asked no questions.

"Thanks." Jayden winked at Jocelyn then brushed a quick kiss on Chloe's cheek before heading down the hall.

"Well, well. My brother sure is smitten with you." Jocelyn sat on the couch and pulled her legs up under her. She patted the couch beside her.

Chloe sat and just stared at Jocelyn. "Smitten with me?"

"Yes. I don't think I have ever seen him this into a female before. I say it's about time someone stole his heart."

"I didn't...I think you have it wrong. He just wants to protect me from some trouble that seems to have found me. There's nothing more than that," Chloe stammered, trying to find a way out of this conversation.

"What kind of trouble?"

"Nothing really. Jayden is making more out of it than is necessary. An old boyfriend trying to reach me, I don't really want to talk to him so..." Chloe drifted off to silence.

"Hmmm. Intriguing, but I have to say it's not like Jayden to make too much out of something. And it certainly isn't like him to bring his work home with him. You are more than a case to him, Chloe."

Chloe leaned against the back of the couch and closed her eyes. "It's just not the right time." Her words were soft and heart wrenching.

"Can I ask you something?" Jocelyn paused.

Chloe opened her eyes. "Sure."

"You appear to like my brother also, so why are you pushing him away? What has you so spooked from a relationship?"

"Relationship? I barely know your brother. I just wanted to start my life over."

"Chloe, I'm a good judge of character and I think you

are perfect for Jayden, but I don't want to see him hurt. So if you are hiding anything, now would be the time to clear the air."

Chloe shook her head. "You two are just alike, suspicious. There's nothing. Bad past, boyfriend causing problems, that's all." The words even sounded phony to her own ears. Jocelyn would never believe her. Subconsciously her hand moved to her stomach and stayed there.

She had to protect this child. No one could know until she moved on. She would contact Carla later and let her know how she was doing. They sat in silence each lost in their own thoughts until Jayden came into the room.

Chloe's breath caught seeing him standing there in bare feet, fresh jeans, and blue t-shirt clinging to his muscles. She couldn't look away. The sound of her heart beating sounded so loud in her ears, drowning out everything around her. She shook her head to equalize her hearing again. She took a deep breath and let it out slowly.

"You okay?" Jayden knelt in front of her, taking both of her hands.

"Yes, of course."

"You got white for a minute. Do you want some water?"

"No, no. I'm fine." She smiled and gave his hands a squeeze. "Stop being so overprotective."

Jocelyn stood. "Let me get some water." She left the room with a questioning glance to Jayden. He had barely shaken his head in response before turning back to Chloe.

"Jayden, you need to stop this." Chloe leaned forward to make sure she had his attention.

"Stop what? Caring for you? Not going to happen." He leaned forward and kissed her gently.

A soft clearing of her voice queued then to Jocelyn's return. She handed Chloe a glass of water. "Want to tell me what is going on, darling brother?"

Jayden glanced at Chloe and as she shook her head no to him, he squeezed her hands. "We need to let her know. She's family, Chloe."

"Jayden, don't do this." Chloe tried to pull her hand back but he held on.

"Please. Let her help us."

"It's not us who need help."

Jayden stood and paced to the other side of the living room. "My God, Chloe, don't do this." His voice was harsh, but as a tear traveled down her cheek he was across the room in a heartbeat. "Don't cry. I'm sorry."

"You called her here, didn't you?" Her voice was soft. She raised a hand to his cheek and ran her thumb slowly back and forth.

He nodded his head. "I'm sorry. I don't know how to reach you. I thought you would talk to her. Chloe, I love you. Please talk to Jocelyn if you won't to me."

Chloe closed her eyes and rested her forehead against Jayden's. "There's too much you don't know. I can't tell you."

"Talk to Jocelyn. You don't have to tell me and she won't tell me, only give me an idea what to do to keep you safe. Trust her Chloe, please."

He kissed her forehead softly as he stood. "I'll be in the other room."

CHAPTER TWENTY-TWO

Tony was in no mood to deal with the incompetence that surrounded him. He had made it clear that Joe wasn't to check in unless he had news on Chloe's whereabouts. Consequently, he hadn't heard from any of his men. He was furious that Chloe had been able to hide from him. He always thought she lacked any kind of street smarts. Apparently he had been very wrong.

She denied hearing anything when questioned, but at this point he couldn't take any chances. Had he believed she didn't know things, he would just let her go and be done with her. Instead now it was a race to find her before she told her police friend things she shouldn't – if she hadn't already.

Tony slammed his hand on the steering wheel. He had been parked out in front of Carla's house since early morning and still no sign of her. She should be leaving to open the diner soon, but instead the house looked empty. With a sigh, he started the vehicle. He'd get coffee at the diner and pressure her a bit more as to Chloe's whereabouts. He was at the end of his patience and just wanted all this behind him.

He was surprised when he pulled around the corner to see Carla opening the diner. Had she been with Chloe. How was it possible? He sat outside her house all night, When did she, how did she? His frustration shot through him. He parked and sat there for a moment. This was a delicate situation. Carla was tougher than he first thought. She wouldn't put up with the bullying, nor would she answer questions readily. He drummed his fingers on the steering wheel.

With a smirk, he exited the vehicle and went inside. He moved to a bench in the back of the diner and gestured for coffee. He kept his eyes on Carla as she made her way to his table with a cup of coffee. "Anything else?"

"I think I will have the special." Tony smiled.

She met his eyes and never blinked. There was no warmth in her face. She gave a brief nod and turned towards the kitchen.

Tony pulled out his cell phone and called Joe. Giving him instructions, he hung up and waited for the food. There was more than one way to get to Chloe. She had a soft heart. He would rely on that to draw her into the open.

Carla slid the plate in front of Tony. "Will that be all?"

"For the moment. Thank you."

* * *

Carla put the check on the table and walked away. She had never turned away business, but in this moment she wanted nothing more than to tell him to go elsewhere. She hadn't heard from Jayden last night and had no idea if he found Chloe. She had stayed the night at the shelter. She and Sarah had been up all night talking. Sarah knew nothing more than what Carla had told her when Chloe moved in.

For the next few hours, Carla was busy with the breakfast crowd. Tony stayed in the booth the whole time, even though she refused to take more coffee to him. During a break, she called Jayden. When he didn't pick up his cell phone, Carla's heart started pounding. What if something had happened to him?

She dialed his home number. After the third ring, Jayden's voice came on the line.

"Where have you been?"

"Carla? I'm sorry I didn't call. It was late when we got back. Chloe's been upset." He sighed.

"Is she okay?"

"Yeah. Jocelyn is here now."

Carla glanced around the diner. It was empty except for Tony and his lackey who had showed up after she delivered his food. "Why can't you just trust her?"

The frustration came through the phone. "Why don't you tell me?"

"It's not my place, Jay. She needs to do this in her own timing." Carla was silent for a moment. "Have you told her yet?"

"Told her what?"

"How you feel." Carla waited, holding her breath.

"Yeah. There wasn't much response except that she said I didn't want to be involved with her." Carla could hear Jayden pacing. "I'm a fool, aren't I?"

"No. I believe she's worth it, Jay. Hang in there. Give her my love. I've got to run." Carla hung up as Tony stood from the table.

He placed the check and cash by the register on his way out. Carla didn't move until he was gone. As she gathered the money to put into the register, an envelope with Chloe's name sat under the check. It was sealed. She slid it into her pocket.

CHAPTER TWENTY-THREE

Chloe sat there with her eyes closed. How much could she tell Jocelyn? Could she—should she—tell her everything? The weight of the world was on her shoulders and she was going under. Life would be so much easier if she hadn't met Jayden, yet she couldn't imagine her life without him at this point. She needed him, wanted him to hold her and tell her it was alright and that she was safe. She wanted his security and his love. *Love.* She never thought she would have that kind of love her parents had. For the first time ever she had a strong desire, and hope, that it could happen. She could envision Jayden being a father to her child, maybe wanting more children.

"Chloe?" Jocelyn's soft voice broke through her thoughts.

Chloe glanced over at Jocelyn and took a deep breath. "What has Jayden told you?"

"Not much, except your boyfriend is trying to get to you, and he's not a very nice man." Jocelyn paused. "Do you want to talk about it? Don't be pressured by Jayden to tell me anything you aren't comfortable talking about."

"I have been on my own for so long. It's hard to trust people, but I want to trust Jayden." Chloe tucked her feet under her on the couch and faced Jocelyn.

"He is the most trustworthy guy I know, and I'm not just saying that because he is my brother." She smiled. "I have worried about him for a long time now. I didn't think he would ever give himself the chance to feel love and really live again. I guess I should thank you. Despite your misgivings, you are the best thing that has come into his life."

Chloe shook her head. "I don't know how. I'm a mess, my life, my emotions...I can't think straight when he is around. I want..."

Jocelyn stood from the chair and moved to the couch. Sitting in front of Chloe, she grabbed her hands. "What do you want, Chloe? It's just you and me."

She blinked back a tear and squeezed Jocelyn's hand. "I want to be able to love him, to allow him to give me the safety he wants."

"So let him in." The words were just a whisper, but it was the break in the damn that brought the tears streaming down Chloe's face.

They sat in silence while Chloe let the tears fall. The cascade was years of hurt and trying to be strong that had finally gave away to possible hope. As Chloe took a deep breath and calmed, Jocelyn stood and left the room. She returned with a box of Kleenex and once again sat close on the couch facing Chloe.

"Ready to talk now?"

Chloe nodded yes. "It's been so long since someone has cared."

"I imagine it has. From what I have gathered, you have been on your own, and being as strong as anyone could be for the circumstances you were in. There's no guilt in getting out of a bad situation."

"It's more than that." Chloe rolled the Kleenex in her hand. "I had to get out because it's not just me anymore."

Jocelyn's face went from unsure to a smile taking over. "How far along are you?"

"Almost five months. Jayden doesn't know." Panic brought her voice up a notch.

"He doesn't have to right now. I think you need to tell him pretty soon, or else he is going to notice anyway, but right now we need to think about your safety."

"I didn't want to lie to him, but I...he couldn't possibly want to be with someone like me."

"Someone like you? What do you mean?" Jocelyn sat a little straighter. "I can assure you my brother will think no different of you when he finds out."

"I didn't mean to imply he wasn't a good person. I just don't know how he would react, and I certainly don't expect that he'll want to be involved with me."

"You're being a bit unfair, aren't you?" Jocelyn spoke harshly. Taking a deep breath, she continued. "He wouldn't feel an obligation, but he does obviously have feelings for you. That isn't going to change because of your circumstances."

Chloe stood and paced the living room. "So what is it that he wants to do? Regarding Tony? I will not continue to run away. I need to face him."

"You don't really believe that putting yourself in danger is going to solve anything?"

"I think it's time to take my life back and that doesn't mean hiding behind Jayden. Tony will never stop until I stand up to this."

"That's insane, Chloe. Think of the baby."

Chloe faced Jocelyn. "No talk of the baby. I know how to protect my child." The moment of weakness and crying had passed. Chloe straightened her back. "I've got this. Please you and Jayden need to leave it alone."

"Wow. Really? You are going to go the 'I'm stronger than anyone else' route on this? I like you a lot and I'm worried. Don't push us away at a time like this." She stood. "I will respect your wishes to a point, but I won't let you do what you're planning."

* * *

Jocelyn turned and walked out of the living room. She shook her head and yet respected Chloe's determination to take care of herself. She found Jayden out on the deck. She stood in the kitchen and watched her brother. The dark circles under his eyes were evidence of his concern, although they were faint. He had been through plenty, and she knew he still fought his demons over the shooting. It would devastate him if something happened to Chloe, and Jocelyn wondered if he would ever heal from it.

Pulling the door open, she stepped onto the deck. "Hey."

"Is she okay?"

"She is one tough cookie. That's strength, Jay, even if you don't think so right now."

"What did she say?"

Jocelyn dropped into a chair across from him. "I'm not sure. I think you might have to let her do it her way."

"No. Not an option."

"Jay, you can't control the outcome here. She's strong, but she needs to do things her way." Jocelyn smiled. "She's a bit stubborn. Does that remind you of anyone?"

Jayden smirked. "I can be more stubborn. I can't let anything happen to her."

"This isn't the past. Chloe isn't a child."

"What gives, Joce? Are you telling me to back off?"

"I'm telling you to not push her. Let her come to you for the help."

"No. I can't let her just disappear." Jayden ran his fingers through his hair.

"You can't keep her here. Jay, think about this."

"I can't let her go either."

Jocelyn looked up to see Chloe in the door watching them. She gestured for her to join them.

* * *

"I see it in your eyes, Jayden. I don't want to be stuck here, hidden away. I left to get my life back." Chloe took a deep breath. "Can we find a compromise on this?"

"What do you want, Chloe? I want you safe."

The corners of her mouth turned up slightly. "I want to be safe too, but I can't hide anymore. I have to face him and get it over with."

"No way. I won't let your put yourself in danger."

"You won't *let* me...Jayden?." Chloe sat back in the chair.

"Trust you like you trust me, Chloe? Don't you think it has to go both ways?"

Jocelyn stood. "I think you two have a lot to talk about. Keep me posted." She leaned over and hugged Chloe close. "You need to trust him."

The words were just a whisper for Chloe only. Chloe gave her a squeeze and nodded. They sat in silence until Jocelyn was gone.

Chloe took a deep breath and blew it out slowly. "I don't know what to say, Jayden, but please let me try to explain without interruptions."

"Okay."

"You know I have been in this terrible situation for far too long, and yes, I ran to try and put some distance between me and Tony. It wasn't the right way to handle it, but I had to do it that way for reasons, one I'm not ready to tell you about. But know this, because of you I have the strength to face him. I need to. It's the only way to get rid of these fears of mine forever." She paused, watching him. "Why do you feel the need to hide me away?"

Jayden sat forward, his hands clenched together with his chin resting on them. "I used to work in Portland on the police force. There was an incident that changed my life forever and I'm afraid I won't be able to protect you if

I have to." He drew in a shaky breath. "I'm afraid I will let you down."

Of all the things he could have said, it was the one that made Chloe's heart skip a beat. He was afraid to let her down. No one had ever thought they would let her down. No one had ever cared that much for her before. The tears threatened to spill again, but she was able to blink them away.

"How could you possibly let me down?"

"Chloe, if anything happens to you I could never forgive myself."

"You can't control things, Jayden."

He chuckled. "Guess that makes me a bit of a control freak."

"I will make you a promise. I will try to trust you and talk with you about things, but you have to stop hiding me away. I have a job at the diner and I need to get back to work."

"No." Jayden stood and walked over to the railing.

Chloe followed him and laid her hand on his arm. "Jayden." Her soft voice turned him towards her. He met her gaze and leaned down, gently brushing his lips against hers. He wrapped his arm around her waist and pulled her close. Gentleness gave way to more demanding as she leaned into him. A soft moan escaped her and Jayden pulled back.

"I do love you, Chloe. Let me in your life."

"I don't know what I'm feeling. I know I want this hope of what could be, but I'm scared."

He pulled her close and held her. His strength warmed her. He sighed. "Fine, let's go to the diner to see Carla. But I'm staying while you're there."

"Can you at least just sit at the counter and let me work?" She smiled up at him. Maybe the trust would come...in time.

CHAPTER TWENTY-FOUR

Carla glanced up as the bell above the door rang. She shook her head seeing the two of them walking in.

"What are you doing here?" Asked Carla

Jayden pointed to a booth near the back. "Coffee, please."

Carla grabbed the pot and headed to the booth they sat in. "You're supposed to be out of sight."

Chloe covered her cup. "Milk, please. And no, I'm not hiding. I'm going to have a glass of milk and then I'm going to help you with the customers."

"Oh, no you're not." Carla poured Jayden's coffee. "What about you? What are you doing?"

Jayden looked at Chloe and her heart skipped a beat. "I'm compromising, apparently. She doesn't want to hide away."

"Tony was here looking for you this morning. He left this." Carla slid the envelope across the table to Chloe. "I'll get your milk."

Chloe picked up the envelope. She turned it over noting it was sealed.

"Are you going to open it?"

"Not yet."

Jayden sipped his coffee. She could tell by the grip on his cup that he held his tongue. Chloe needed to be in control of this. He sighed. Patience was never his strong suit and she knew this was killing him.

"I can't open it right now."

"I know. When you're ready."

Chloe laughed. "You're dying over there and I know it, but thanks."

Carla returned with the glass of milk and slid into the booth next to Chloe. "Well, what did it say?"

"I haven't opened it."

Carla stared at Jayden. He shrugged his shoulders. She turned towards Chloe. "What are you waiting for?"

"Well, I'm thinking there are some customers who need waiting on and you probably need a break." She drank down the milk and slid against Carla. "Let me get up and I'll get to work."

* * *

Carla stood and let Chloe out. She waited until Chloe went into the kitchen before sitting back down. "What's going on?"

Jayden smiled. "Chloe is calling the shots. She doesn't want to hide from Tony any longer."

"And you're okay with that?"

"No, not really, but if I push too hard she will shut me out and I need to be here beside her. It's the only way I will be able to protect her."

"Protect her by putting her right in harm's way?"

"Look, I feel the way you do, but you know as well as I do if it was you, you would do exactly the same thing as Chloe. You would want to face your fears and stop running. She thinks it is the only way to get her life back, and she's probably right about that."

Carla shook her head. "I don't like it, Jay."

"I know. Neither do I."

He glanced over and watched Chloe interacting with the customers. Her face lit up and she truly enjoyed the people she talked with. She was so beautiful and it startled him with the intensity of feelings he had for her already.

"Did she talk with Jocelyn?"

"I think so. Joce didn't tell me anything, except I needed to back off and let her face her fears."

Carla stared at him. "You're kidding? And you're listening? What is it that I'm missing in all of this?"

"What do you mean?"

"You seem all of a sudden too laid back. You must have something up your sleeve."

Jayden shook his head. "No, nothing. I'm trying to trust her." He played with the coffee cup. "I still have nightmares about Portland and I don't want anything to happen to her, but one thing Joce is right about – I can't control any outcome no matter how many scenarios I play through in my mind."

CHAPTER TWENTY-FIVE

Chloe closed her eyes as she sat back in Jayden's car. She was tired after working at the diner, yet content with the fact that she was being proactive. She had expected Tony to show up at any point throughout the day, but he hadn't. And Jayden was true to his word, staying in sight at all times.

All day her mind had been on this evening and how it would be with Jayden. He had already told her he loved her. She needed to tell him about the baby, but just couldn't bring herself to.

"Tired?"

Chloe opened her eyes and glanced at Jayden. He smiled at her. "A little, but it feels good to have done something today."

"I'll cook dinner and you can rest, if you want."

"That sounds good, but you're spoiling me. I should be cooking for you."

Jayden smiled as he kept his eyes on the road. "I enjoy cooking and never get to cook for others. This is a treat for me."

She nodded slightly as she drifted into a light sleep. Her mind was full of Tony and wondering about the note he had left her. She had yet to read it, but her mind was filled with the worst-case scenario, racing with thoughts of Tony catching her and the baby being hurt.

"Chloe?"

She roused slowly and opened her eyes. Seeing Jayden, feeling his hand on her arm, she calmed. "Just a bad dream."

"Tony?"

"Yeah, I guess that with everything that is happening he is on my mind." She sighed.

"It's understandable. It's on all our minds." He gave her arm a gentle squeeze before moving it back to the steering wheel. The arm immediately cooled where his hand had been and the longing for him to touch her again startled her.

"I need for this to be done with."

"Did you read his note?" Jayden asked.

"No, not yet."

"Will you tell me what it says?" Jayden glanced over for her reaction.

"If it is relevant to what is going on." She was purposefully vague and he didn't like it, but couldn't argue with her. Blind trust rubbed him the wrong way. He wanted to draw her close into his arms and never let her go. She was not ready for that, holding him at arm's length, but at times he had held her she was so inviting and warm. Confusion clouded his mind and he shook his head.

"Everything okay?" Chloe was watching him.

"Fine. A long day." Jayden pulled into his driveway. "Let's get some food and just relax tonight."

They entered the house and Jayden gestured to the living room. "I'll get dinner. Go put your feet up."

"I'm going to shower first, if that's okay. Then get comfy."

Jayden headed to the kitchen. She was sure his mind full of scenarios of what Tony's note could possibly say. But she had to find out what was in it first, before she knew if she could share it.

Chloe ran the water in the shower and stood under the warm spray, tension ebbing from her body. Her legs were tired from being on her feet all day. She splayed her fingers across her belly and felt the gentle flutter. It was the second time she had felt that type of motion. It had to be the baby moving. She stood still. The motion was gone as quick as it started, but it was enough – enough to give her hope for the future and her new life with a child.

She toweled off and slipped into some sweatpants and a baggy sweatshirt. In the guest bedroom, she sat on the edge of the bed and stared at the envelope. It was now or never. She slowly ripped open the end and pulled out the sheet of paper.

Meet me at the diner tomorrow at 9 p.m. Come alone and you won't get hurt. Don't tell your police friend or it will be the last time you see or hear from him.

She read it and reread it. She would be a fool to meet him alone. This may have been the opportunity she wanted, but did she have the courage to go through with it? She tucked the note back into the envelope and slid it into her purse. She stood straight and squared her shoulders. Now to convince Jayden she hadn't read it.

Chloe curled up on the end of the couch and thumbed through a magazine. She wished she had a good book to read, something lighthearted with a happily ever after. Jayden came in with two plates.

"Looks good." Chloe reached for the plate. There was an omelet loaded with broccoli, mushrooms, and cheese, along with an English muffin and fruit. She bit into her first forkful and closed her eyes. *Heaven.*

"That good, huh?" Jayden chuckled.

"Delicious. Thank you."

They made small talk while eating. Pushing the plates onto the coffee table, Jayden reached for Chloe's feet. "Here, let me rub your feet. They must be killing you after being on them all day."

"You don't have to do that." Chloe spoke, although stretching out her legs towards him. She sighed as he massaged her feet. She could get used to this. "You spoil me."

"Is that a bad thing?"

"No, but it's unrealistic to think this could last." Chloe didn't have to open her eyes to know the impact her words had on Jayden. He had professed his love for her and although she felt it, she couldn't say the words.

"It doesn't have to be unrealistic, Chloe."

She opened her eyes and watched him. "Jayden, there is too much unspoken. It can't be overcome."

"That's your opinion and the decision you're making alone. Why can't you let me in and let me decide what I can handle, and what I can't?"

Chloe closed her eyes tight, willing the tears not to fall. How she wanted to believe him. She was so relaxed with him and deep in her heart she knew Jayden would never hurt her. Yet, she kept holding back. If she survived the meeting with Tony, she would tell Jayden everything.

CHAPTER TWENTY-SIX

Jayden massaged Chloe's feet, feeling the tension leave her. He knew the moment she fell into a peaceful rest. His hand stilled, but never left her foot. He laid his head back and closed his eyes. At least he could be close to her while they slept. He had no idea how to get her to open up.

He slowly opened his eyes to the warmth of Chloe snuggled close; her head was on his chest, her arm wrapped around his middle. Jayden's arm was over her shoulder and held her close. He sighed softly. At least in slumber she opened up on some level.

He slowly ran his fingers down her arm and marveled at the softness. He stilled as she stirred against him. Glancing down at her, his eyes met hers as he found her watching him. "Morning," he whispered.

"Morning yourself." She snuggled closer.

"Sleep well?"

"I did, but I think you will have a crick in your neck the way you were all night. I should have woke you so you could have gone to bed, but I just wanted to be close."

"I'm fine. I loved holding you." His fingers ran lightly up and down her arm. "Did the note frighten you?" He held his breath hoping her answer wasn't yes, but that she wanted to be with him.

Chloe pushed away and sat up. "Maybe a little." She shook her head to clear her thoughts. He was ever the protector. She couldn't tell if it was out of his vows to protect and serve that he stayed close or was it because he professed to love her. She wanted clarity of the situation.

"What are you thinking, Chloe?" Jayden stared at her with such intensity she felt he could see right down to her soul.

"Honestly? I can't read you at all." Chloe replied.

He smiled. "Well that makes two of us." He leaned toward her and held her chin in his hand. He paused just before touching her lips with his. "Chloe, I love you. I mean it. Don't have doubts." Before she could respond his lips brushed hers with a gentleness she had never experienced.

Just as quickly as the kiss started, Jayden ended it and stood. "Coffee?"

Chloe paled. "Nothing for me right now. I'm going to change and wash up."

Jayden, puzzled, started for the kitchen to make coffee. He shook his head as he struggled to know her, how to get her to trust him. He had to work today and didn't want her alone. He pulled out his cell phone and sent a quick text to Carla asking if she could keep an eye on Chloe at the diner.

His mood improved as Carla confirmed that she would keep Chloe close. Leaning against the counter, Jayden sipped his coffee. He was lost in thought and startled when he realized Chloe was in the door of the kitchen watching him.

"Feel better?"

"Yeah, thanks."

"Want some breakfast?"

"No, not now. I'll grab something at the diner." Chloe took a step closer and stopped. "Can you give me a ride?"

Jayden nodded. "Let me just get changed. I've got to work today, but you know how to reach me if you need anything."

CHAPTER TWENTY-SEVEN

Tony sat in his car and watched Carla and Chloe go into the diner. So she was back. He chuckled to himself thinking how easy she had made it for him. He wasn't sure the level of her betrayal, but it would be determined as soon as he was alone with her.

He knew from his sources that Jayden was working today. He probably would be showing up at the diner at some point to check on Chloe. Tony would have to move as soon as the diner was closed. At that time she would be alone for a little bit. He sat back and closed his eyes. Waiting was all he could do right now.

* * *

Chloe paused inside the door to the diner. "Did you see him out there?"

Carla turned and looked out the window. "Tony?"

"Yes."

"I didn't see him. We probably should let Jayden know."

Chloe shook her head. "No. He won't do anything right now. Let's just get ready for the day."

* * *

Carla acknowledged her. As customers started pouring in, she put Jayden from her mind and just enjoyed having the help today. Summer was over and it was all local people here now. In some ways, Carla preferred the off-season when she had a chance to just interact with the locals.

Chloe worked hard, but Carla saw her sitting whenever she had a free moment. She had gotten out of the routine the little bit of time off from waitressing and Carla knew the pregnancy was starting to be a factor. She wondered if Chloe had told Jayden yet. There was a bit of a bump that showed when Chloe wore her apron, but not knowing about the pregnancy, anyone would think she was just gaining a little weight and looking healthy.

The day passed quickly as locals talked about the upcoming winter season storms and the Farmer's Almanac. Chloe laughed and talked with everyone like she was one of their own. Carla wasn't surprised when late in the afternoon the door opened and Jayden walked in for coffee.

"I expected you here sooner," Carla teased.

"She's in good hands with you." Jayden sipped his coffee, his eyes never leaving Chloe.

"How'd it go last night?"

Jayden glanced at Carla. "She was relaxed and slept well, if that's what you mean." He sighed. "She's still keeping me at arm's length. I don't know how to get through to her."

"You don't. She'll come around." Carla leaned on the counter. "Tony was sitting outside when we got here this morning."

"I figured. He's still there." Jayden played with the mug. "Can you get back to my place without him tailing you?"

"I don't see why not. Where's David in all this?"

"He's following up a lead in Portland for me. He should be back tonight."

Carla nodded.

Jayden turned on his stool as Chloe joined them and sat next to him. "Long day?"

"Yeah, but it feels good to be out and doing something instead of hiding away."

Jayden nodded and Carla smiled. *He looks happy, something she hasn't seen in a long time.* "You're looking tired again. I thought you slept good?"

"I did. Just not used to being on my feet, I guess. I'm fine. Stop hovering."

"I am not hovering. Just stopped in for coffee."

Chloe winked. "Yeah, you keep telling yourself that."

"Are you complaining?"

Chloe's cheeks turned pink. "Not at all."

Carla smirked. "You can take off now if you want, Chloe. I'm sure Jayden can drive you to his place. I will be along in an hour after I close up."

Jayden glared at Carla.

"That's sounds good." Chloe stood, untying her apron. "Do you mind, Jayden, or are you busy working?"

"I'm not too busy to drive you home, but I can't stay and I would prefer you not be alone."

"It's an hour. What can it hurt?" Chloe stood with her hands on her hips.

Jayden stared at Carla. "Really? You want to explain that to her?"

Carla shrugged. "An hour, Jayden…what can happen?"

Jayden ran his fingers through his hair. "A lot can happen in an hour. He's sitting right out there and will follow us. Come to the station with me, Chloe. Carla can pick you up there."

"I might as well stay here and work then. Can't you just trust me for one hour?"

Jayden sighed. "It's not you I don't trust, it's him. Can't you see that?"

Chloe laid her hand on his arm. "Jayden, please. I can't hide behind you and Carla for the rest of my life."

"Why not? I'm happy to protect you the rest of your life."

Chloe shook her head. "Please, don't go there."

Jayden closed his eyes and took a deep breath. "Fine. I'll be in the car and will drive you home when you are ready."

She squeezed his arm. "Thanks."

* * *

Chloe watched Carla as Jayden left. His concern and peace overwhelmed her when he was close. She needed to get through this by herself. Part of her hoped Tony would try something when she was alone before she had to make a decision about meeting him, get it over with so she could either move on or...she shuddered at the thought of what he could do to her.

"You okay?" Carla's voice broke her train of thought.

"Yeah."

"You don't have to do this."

"I have to, Carla. I will never be through with this until Tony makes a move."

"Chloe, you're purposely hoping he comes for you?" Carla's eyes grew large.

"I don't think he will with me being at Jayden's house. Please, keep it to yourself. I have a feeling Jayden won't go too far."

"Chloe, that's not fair to Jayden. Have you told him about the baby yet?"

Chloe looked down at her hands. "No, I haven't. I don't know how to bring it up. He's so overprotective right now and I don't want him to feel obligated."

"He loves you. Can't you see that?"

Chloe met Carla's eyes. "Yes, I see it. I feel it every time he is close by. I need to get through this thing with Tony before I can even think about that."

"You love him too, don't you?"

"I don't know. I'm not sure I would recognize what love is at this point. I know I want to be with him, I love the warmth and security when I am near him. But I don't want to jump into another situation where I can't be in control of my own life, Carla. I need to get through this thing, whatever it is, with Tony."

"I understand that, and Jayden would too."

Chloe shook her head. "Please, let me work through this my own way."

"To what end? I can't bear the thought of something happening to you or your baby."

"You think I can?" Chloe trembled. "I can't lose this baby. It's my whole life."

Carla took a deep breath. "Chloe, I've been there. Don't try to do this on your own."

"Come over when you're done working and we can talk some more then."

CHAPTER TWENTY-EIGHT

Jayden sat in his car watching Tony watching the diner. He knew Tony would follow them and didn't know if he could leave her at the house alone. He picked up his phone and punched in Dave's number.

"How far away are you?" He jumped right to the point as soon as Dave answered.

"Just leaving now. Will be there in about an hour. What's up?"

Jayden cursed under his breath. "I have to work and Chloe is insisting on being at the house by herself."

"Call Joce and get her over there." Dave paused before he continued. "The word is that he thinks Chloe related his dealings to you. He will kill her if he gets his hands on her."

Jayden closed his eyes. "I can't protect her, Dave."

"You can and you will. This isn't the same situation, Jay. Come on, man. Get a grip."

"There is more than she's telling me. Maybe she *does* know something. If she would just open up we could arrest him at least on stalking charges."

"I think I have enough to do that, but don't let him near her. It will have to wait until I get there."

Jayden sighed. "Here she comes. Call me as soon as you're close."

"Gotcha. Bye."

Jayden put down his phone as Chloe opened the door. "All set?"

Chloe buckled her seat belt and turned towards him. "Yes. Thank you for doing this."

Jayden watched her carefully. "I don't think I can do it, Chloe. I just can't leave you alone."

She reached for his hand. "Please, Jayden, I need to do this."

"He's dangerous. What is it that he thinks you have betrayed him on?"

"Betrayed him? I don't know. Tony doesn't always think logically, in fact he rarely thinks things through before he reacts."

Jayden sighed. "Which makes him even more dangerous. Can't you see he is going to come after you when you are alone?"

"Jayden..." She closed her eyes. She had to tell him. "I don't know how..."

Jayden released her hand and started the car. He put it in gear and started towards home. He kept one eye on the rearview mirror and watched Tony pull out behind them.

Chloe's mind raced. She wanted to tell him, but it caught in her throat. He needed to know before he continued to profess his love for her. He would want to be rid of her, carrying another man's child. He wouldn't want to take that on. A lone tear slipped from her eye and coursed its way down her cheek. She closed her eyes and wished her parents were still alive. Her mother would know what to tell her.

Jayden pulled into his driveway and shut off the car. "Chloe."

She glanced at him. "Are you staying?"

"We need to talk. I know you have things you haven't said, and either don't want to tell me or don't know how. It's time to get it all out in the open."

"Jayden, it's not that easy."

"Of course it is. Let's go in. Tony's right down the street."

Chloe glanced around. "He followed you?"

"Of course. Did you think he wouldn't?"

Chloe trembled as they started in. Jayden's hand on her lower back was a welcome warmth. As soon as the door shut behind them, Jayden pulled her into his arms. "Chloe, talk to me."

She wrapped her arms around his waist and held tight. She could feel his breath on her neck as he held her close. "Jayden, I'm afraid."

She looked up and met his eyes. The love that shone from his dark eyes gave her courage. She pulled away and hanging onto his hand walked to the living room.

She sat on the couch and gestured for him to sit next to her.

She was silent as Jayden waited. It was killing him to be patient, but she wracked her brain how to start.

"I care for you, Jayden, I do. You tell me you love me and it scares me. I don't know how to love. I've never been in love." She paused and still he was silent. His hand held hers and his thumb rubbed encouragingly over her palm.

"I don't know what Tony thinks I told you. I know he is into things that are illegal, but I don't know the details of anything. He must think I do, but I really don't. I have tried very hard to stay away from anything that would give me information. I didn't want to know. I thought I would be safe if I didn't."

"You're not safe, though, Chloe. As long as you're alive, he will feel you're a threat. I can't live with the thought that I could lose you."

Chloe sighed. "I know. I left because I thought I could protect myself and disappear from him."

"Protect yourself from what…if you don't know anything?"

Chloe gripped his hand tighter. "Jayden, I understand after I tell you this that it is a very real possibility you are going to walk out that door and have nothing to do with me. I don't blame you."

"Let me decide that, please, Chloe."

She took a deep breath and let it out slowly. "Jayden…"

Jayden's cell phone rang, "Hang on." He stood and walked to the window to look out. Tony's car was still there. Jayden listened carefully and swore softly as Dave told him he had been hung up in Portland and would be a little later getting there.

"I can't reach Joce. It will take Carla at least an hour to get here."

"Can't help it, man. Tell her to lock up and stay put." Dave paused. "I can't fill you in now, but Tony's there alone. Joe's in Portland."

"Okay. Let me know when you're back."

CHAPTER TWENTY-NINE

Jayden walked to the couch and sat down. The tears that coursed down Chloe's face broke his heart. Whatever it was, she was scared. His stomach clenched with anticipation, his mind racing with worse case scenarios yet the only thing that would separate him from her death. He wanted her beside his side forever, no matter what the secrets were. The realization of the depth of his love startled him.

He reached for her hand and squeezed it. He waited for her to speak.

She wiped the tears from her cheeks, took a deep breath and faced him. "I left Tony because I needed a better life."

"I know."

"No, I needed a better life for...my baby." She watched his face as he absorbed the words she was saying.

"Is this the part that is supposed to make me run?" Jayden smiled. "A baby is a blessing, Chloe. I'm not afraid of responsibility."

"But it's not your responsibility. It's mine."

"Hey." His voice was soft. "Yes, it's your responsibility and you are going to be a great mother. You're already putting your baby ahead of any of your needs, but I'm not running, Chloe. I would love if you let me help you with this, be a part of your life, and the baby's."

The tears started again as his words impacted her. "Are you sure?"

"Yes, positive. I love you. I don't know how else to convey that to you." He pulled her close and kissed her lips softly. His lips caressed hers with a gentleness she didn't think was possible.

He stepped back from her, realizing the shadows in the room indicated how late it was getting. "I need to get to the station to finish up some things. Carla should be here any minute. Please stay in the house and keep it locked. Don't open the door for anyone unless you know it's Carla."

"I know. I'm fine." Chloe gave him a slight push. "Go."

* * *

She sank into the couch. The burden lifted, and her spirits were high. She rubbed her belly, feeling so blessed to have met Jayden. He hadn't even flinched at the news. What a fool she had been to think he would. With a smile on her face, she slipped in a light sleep.

A knock on the door brought her sitting straight up. Tony? No he wouldn't knock. It must be Carla. She glanced at the clock and saw that a half hour had passed since Jayden left. She jumped up and ran to the door.

Looking through the peephole, she saw Carla standing there. She swung it open and found Tony to the side, out of view of the peephole.

"Miss me?" Tony smirked and pushed Carla inside. He glanced around outside before shutting the door behind him.

"What are you doing here?" Chloe grabbed Carla and held her close.

"I'm here for you, my dear. Did you really think you could just walk out of my life and get involved with a police officer?"

"We're not involved." Chloe's eyes ran over Tony. She couldn't see a weapon, but that didn't mean there wasn't one.

"Well, I guess you will need to convince me of that." He pushed her and Carla towards the living room. "Why don't you have a seat and let me know all about it."

"I can't do this anymore, Tony. We didn't have a relationship, it was a dictatorship."

Tony chuckled. "Poor little girl. I have been the only one there for you. You've got no one else."

"That's not true. I don't need you. I can take care of myself." Chloe stood, fists clenched beside her.

"Give it a rest, Chloe. You couldn't take care of a dog, and certainly can't take care of yourself. You would have died a long time ago if it wasn't for me."

Chloe's mind raced with what to do. He must have seen Jayden leave. She glanced at Carla who was glaring at Tony.

"Come on. We're getting out of here." Tony grabbed for Chloe's hand. Carla pushed between them.

"You're not taking her."

With the back of his hand, Tony smacked the side of her mouth with enough force to send Carla to the couch.

"Stop!" Chloe pulled at his arm. "I'll go, but leave her alone. Don't hurt her."

"So protective of our friends, are we?"

"Please, Tony. Leave her alone." Chloe stood in front of him.

"Wow. I'm impressed. Suddenly so brave and fearless." Tony snickered and yanked her close. She stiffened as he ran his tongue along her earlobe. "Let's go, Chloe. See if you can save yourself as well as you save your friends."

He pushed her in front of him towards the front door, but turned back. His eyes flickered over Carla on the couch. "Phone lines are cut. Give me your car keys and your cell phone." He reached out a hand.

With hands shaking, Carla did as he asked. "Don't do this."

"You have a ways to walk to reach lover boy. We'll be long gone by then." He turned towards Chloe. "Move."

Tony shoved Chloe into the back seat before jumping into the driver's seat and starting the car. He watched her through the rearview mirror and she knew he saw a changed woman. There was no fear on her face or in her eyes anymore.

"You know he'll never find you in time," he sneered.

"I'm not worried about it. I don't need Jayden to save me, Tony. I'm not afraid of you. You have no hold on me anymore."

"Wow, sweetie. I'm impressed. Where did this sudden backbone come from? The baby?"

Chloe stared at him through the rearview mirror. "How…"

"Yes, I have ways that I know things. You weren't going to tell me?"

"No. I wasn't. This is my baby."

Tony snickered. "Your baby? Honey, you're a child yourself. You would never be able to raise a child by yourself."

Chloe raised her chin and met his gaze. "Don't be so sure."

Tony picked up his cell phone and punched in a number. "Meet me as planned. I have her." He hung up without waiting for an answer.

"Where are we going?" Chloe asked.

"You'll see. Don't worry, lover boy will find you soon enough. Just don't think he'll be in time."

CHAPTER THIRTY

Dave knew what this trip to Portland would cost Jayden. However, it would be good for him to face his fears head-on so he could move past them. His mind wandered to that fateful night that Jayden, and he were involved in the incident. They had been partners then. Jayden always went by the book where Dave had tended to push the envelope a time or two. They made a good team. That night the perp had been running from them. They finally had him cornered when Jayden had his gun drawn on him. The perp had fired, forcing Jayden to return fire just as a child ran out from behind a car. The bullet hit the boy in the back.

The perp had been apprehended, but Jayden never moved from holding the young boy in his arms long after back-up had arrived. It was ruled accidental and Jayden had been cleared to return to duty, but he never did. He handed in his resignation and went back to Arden. Dave had been pleased when he took the Chief of Police position in Arden, but knew it was the safe job for Jayden. In his gut, he knew Jayden needed the adrenaline rush like they all did. After Jayden had left the Portland force, Dave had resigned also and moved into PI work.

Dave was startled when blinding lights hit his rearview mirror. The car was coming on him fast. It was too dark to see the car. He hit the gas to try and put some distance between them, but the car kept coming, gaining second by second. He braced himself for the impact. The car hit him hard. He used all his strength to stay on the road. He glanced in the rearview mirror to see the car pull back, only to see it come at him again.

"Dammit." Dave braked briefly at a sharp curve. He was hit hard again. The car slid on the gravel at the edge of the road. He managed to stop at the edge of the embankment as the car passed. Dave took a deep breath and reached for the cell phone, jumping from the car as the lights turn around and headed back. Sliding behind the brush at the end of the road, he sucked in a few deep breaths.

The car raced towards his vehicle and hit it hard, sending it over the embankment. Dave held his gun in front of him, waiting to see if anyone exited the vehicle. Instead the car backed up and drove off. No plate was on it and it was too dark to see the make and model. He swore softly.

He pulled out his cell and punched in Jayden's number. "You back?"

Dave shook his head. "No, not yet. A bit of a problem. I'm carless. Want to come get me?"

"What happened?"

"Was run off the road. I'm assuming Joe, but couldn't make out the car enough to be positive. I got out of the car before whoever it was came back and pushed it over the embankment."

Jayden swore. "I'll be right there."

"Cliff Road, about halfway along. I'll start walking."

"I'll call Chloe while I'm on my way. Carla should have gotten there by now."

"Make it fast. I don't look forward to walking all the way back to Arden when it's only about a half hour ride." Dave disconnected and slipped his phone into his pocket. It was too dark to get down to his car. With a sigh, he turned toward Arden and started walking.

CHAPTER THIRTY-ONE

Carla waited until the car started and raced to the kitchen. She pulled out drawers until she came to the one that had the station walkie-talkie.

"Jayden, are you there?"

Silence met her.

"Jayden?"

She paced around the living room wondering if Chloe had a cell phone that she didn't take. Carla headed towards her bedroom to search. The walkie-talkie was silent except for occasional static. She found Chloe's purse and rifled through it. She came across a cell phone that was powered off and hit the On button.

"Jayden?" She spoke into the walkie-talkie again. Still no answer. She heaved it on the bed. What good were they if no one answered?

With the phone powered up, she punched in Jayden's cell number. As soon as he answered, she said, "He has her."

"Carla?"

"Yes, it's me. Tony grabbed her. I don't know where they were going. I have no keys or cell phone, but found Chloe's phone." Silence met her. "Jayden?"

"Yes, I'm here. Dammit, how did he get her?"

"Look, Jayden, I'm not happy about it and I am sporting a bruise across my right cheek to prove it. Find her and send someone to get me." She hung up before the tears started falling. She had failed her friend. She lost her child due to a violent man and now she was going to lose Chloe, and her child. The sobs racked her body as the tears flowed.

* * *

Jayden was bombarded with fear and anxiety, then anger. Good, at least he was getting mad. That was a good sign that he would be able to reaction with instinct instead of letting emotions get in the way.

"I'm on my way to pick up Dave. Apparently he's had a bit of car trouble." Jayden sighed.

Jayden floored the gas pedal and made record time to Cliff Road. He came upon Dave about five miles from town. With Dave in the car, he turned back towards town. "Tony's got Chloe."

"Where do we look?"

Jayden looked up. "I have no idea. Where would he take her?"

"My guess would be he would keep her close. He wants you to know he's in control." He turned and faced Jayden. "Can you do this?"

"Yes. I'll do anything to keep her safe."

"Good. Let's go. We'll pick up Carla and then go from there."

The drive to Jayden's house was silent, both David and Jayden in their own thoughts. Carla was on the steps waiting for them.

"What happened?" Jayden demanded as soon as they exited the vehicle.

"He was waiting here when I got here. He got the jump on me, had a gun. Chloe opened the door for me and he was behind me." Carla watched Jayden. "I shouldn't have come here."

"If you hadn't been here it would have been longer before we knew she was gone. It's not your fault." Jayden pulled her into his arms and held her close. "We'll get her back."

Dave interrupted. "Hate to break this up, but any idea where he would have taken her? Did he say anything?"

"He didn't say. I don't know. She was strong though. She stood up to him and didn't show fear. That's a huge step for her."

"I'm afraid her strength will tick him off more. He's used to her being submissive." Jayden ran his fingers through his hair. "Dammit, where would they go?"

"He would want to take her somewhere that would taunt you." Dave was thoughtful. "Where did you see him the most, or interact the most with Chloe in public?"

"It was always the diner."

Dave started to the car. "Then the diner is where we'll start. We can drop Carla off at home on the way."

"I'm not going home."

Jayden shook his head. "You're not going with us. You need to stay home. I'll bring Chloe to you as soon as I can."

"That optimistic?"

"I have to be. It's all I can hold on to right now." Jayden started the car and pulled out, racing for the diner.

Stopping at Carla's house, Jayden stepped out of the cruiser to open the back door. She handed him her key to the diner. "Just in case you need it."

Jayden folded her into a bear hug. "Don't worry. We'll find her."

"Be careful, both of you."

Jayden slid into the car. "Please call Joce and let her know what is going on." He slammed the door and was gone before Carla had turned towards the house.

* * *

Carla let herself in and reached for the phone. She knew Jayden wanted Jocelyn to know for David's sake. Jocelyn had been fighting her feelings for him for as long as Carla could remember. Maybe this was just the thing that would finally knock down her defenses.

Carla minced no words when Jocelyn picked up and filled her on the situation. They agreed she would come to Carla's house and wait for news.

CHAPTER THIRTY-TWO

Tony parked behind an old building next to another car. He rolled down his window to speak with Joe. "PI is out of the picture."

"Good. Now I want you to go back home."

"You might need help with the boyfriend," Joe protested.

Tony shook his head. "This is only going to end one of two ways. I'm either going to jail for a long time or I won't be breathing. You need to get out of here and take over the business."

"What about her?" Joe nodded his head towards the backseat.

Tony glanced over his shoulder. Chloe was huddled against the far door, glaring at him. He sighed. "She'll be fine. I need to find out what information she has given Mr. Police Officer and then I'll dispose of her."

"Disposed of? Just thrown away. Just let me go and you won't need to be bothered with me again."

"Shut up, Chloe." Tony's voice was cold.

She turned towards the window.

"Joe, just get out of here. I'll take care of everything else. If by chance I get past this, I'll catch up with you. If you don't hear from me in the next 24 hours, then move forward with our plans."

"Got it, boss." Joe gave a mock salute and slid into his car.

Tony started his car. He closed his eyes for a moment. Where could he draw Jayden in? If he wasn't going to get through this, he wanted to take the one thing Chloe cared about with him.

"You won't get away with this." Her voice broke through his thoughts.

"You are so sure lover boy is coming for you?" He laughed. "I hope he does and then you can see just want kind of life you created for him."

Chloe shuddered at the callous tone. She had to warn Jayden somehow...but how?

"You have your key for the diner?"

"Yes. Why?"

Tony smiled and turned the car towards town. "I think it is most fitting the place you met him will be the place you say goodbye to him."

"Don't do this, Tony. Please."

"Save it, my dear. I don't care how you feel about him. My one regret will be not being able to take this baby from you. I would have loved a son to leave the family business to."

"I never would have let you near him or her." Her voice rose an octave as her fear grew.

"You say that like you would have had a choice." Tony pulled in behind the diner and shut off the car. "Let's go."

He pulled Chloe from the car and shoved her towards the back door. Her hand shook as she unlocked the door, pushed it open, and stepped inside.

"Far enough. Stay close." Tony locked the door. "Have a seat right there on that stool." He pointed just inside the door.

"What are you going to do now? Jayden will find you here in no time. You had no intention of trying to get away, did you?"

Tony chuckled. "And miss all the fun when he shows up to rescue you? He just won't know what he's stepping into."

Chloe stood and walked towards him. "Don't do this. Nothing happened between him and me. I was just trying to make you jealous. I knew you would come for me." She batted her eyelashes and flashed a smile.

He pushed her back against the stool. "Stop it. You never were very good at seduction, Chloe. You ran from me for no reason and now there are consequences for that."

"I didn't run for no reason. You had no love for me. You wanted a puppet and I couldn't be that anymore. It wasn't fair to the baby."

"A puppet? A puppet would have behaved better than you. All those times I hurt you, you made me do that because you couldn't just be happy with our life."

Chloe stood tall. "I didn't make you do anything. You need help."

He took the gun out of his pocket and placed it on the counter. "Sit down, Chloe. I'm done talking."

"Well I'm not. It's been years, Tony, and I have never said a word to you. I went along with what you wanted, or got beat if I did something wrong. I'm done playing your games. I want out...NOW."

Tony stared at her, his face cold and unemotional. "Well, well. This is a surprise. This new personality of yours would have been quite fun while we were together. Now it bores me."

There was only one door to the outside from here, where they had come in. The other door led to the dining room. It was open. If anyone came in the front the bell would ring so Tony would know. Jayden would be walking into a trap. Chloe had no way to warn him. She wrung her hands. Tony leaned against the counter watching her. As if he could read her thoughts, he smirked. "Don't fret, Chloe. He'll be here soon."

"He won't come alone, you know. You won't make it out alive."

Tony picked up the gun and approached Chloe. "If I don't make it out alive, do you think you will? There will be shots. No one will know whose bullet hit you." He ran the edge of the run down her cheek. "It will be a sweet moment to know he won't have you before I go."

Chloe closed her eyes and took a deep breath. "Don't be so sure of yourself, Tony. Look how long it took you to find me, or even the fact that I was able to get away from you."

He stood straight and put the gun in his belt. "Yes, you are so confident that you fooled me, aren't you?"

* * *

Jayden and David parked just down the road from the diner and crept out of the car, pushing the door shut without a sound. Tony's car had been seen behind the diner as they drove around. "How do you want to do this?" David whispered.

"The problem will be the front door. That stupid bell. No way to open it without the thing making noise. My guess is he has her in the kitchen and there's only one door there."

"So one of us covers the back door while the other opens the front and distracts him." Dave was silent. "I'll take the back if you want."

"He's waiting for me. He's expecting me to come in the front. I don't think he'll try to come out. The question is, who does he want dead more, me or Chloe?"

"Don't think that way. Chloe's smart. She won't push him. We'll get her out."

"Dave...thanks. Take the back and be prepared to get her out of there regardless of what happens."

"Hey, man, are you ready for this?"

"I'm good. I won't let her down."

Dave moved off towards the back of the diner while Jayden went to the front door. There weren't any lights on. He unlocked the door and slid it open as slowly as possible. When he could get his hand in, he grasped the bell while he slipped inside and closed the door. Jayden crept down behind the counter and moved at a snail's pace to the kitchen. At least that door was open.

Chloe was taunting Tony with the fact she had left him. Jayden shook his head. He hoped she wasn't making things worse. Yet the strength in her voice gave him encouragement. This was the woman he wanted to be with, to have a family with. He crept closer to the open door. Tony stood with his back to him.

His gun was pointed at Chloe. Jayden couldn't surprise him and take the chance the gun would go off. He sat back out of sight. He had to somehow signal Chloe he was here.

"Tony, let Chloe go. It will go so much easier for you." Dave's voice broke the silence from the back of the diner.

Jayden peeked around the corner. Tony hauled Chloe against him. He had his gun pointed at her temple.

"She's not coming out. Where is the police chief?"

Jayden stood and moved partially into the door. "I'm right here."

Tony whipped around, bringing Chloe with him. "Clever. Snuck in without the bell ringing. I'm impressed."

"You should be. Now let her go. This is between you and me."

Tony gripped Chloe tighter. "Oh, I think she is a big part of this and should stay."

"You know you can't walk out of here." Jayden's hand trembled. He blinked rapidly to erase the sight of the young boy dying in his arms. This was about Chloe. He wouldn't let her die, not her, not here.

"Having problems with memories?" Tony's taunt broke through Jayden's fog. "Yes, I know all about the young boy you killed. Was considered an accident, but it doesn't feel like it. You are haunted by it all the time, aren't you?"

* * *

Chloe watched Jayden. Tony was hitting a nerve. She knew there had been an incident and he had left the Portland job because of it, but she didn't know it involved a death of a child. The tightness of Jayden's jaw indicated that he had pulled himself into a more focused groove.

She kept her eyes on Jayden, trying to convey to him the strength that he needed. Her life without him flashed before her eyes and she felt warm with the realization that this was what love was – being there for someone when it was tough, no matter what. If they could make it through this, they stood a chance of making a relationship work.

"Let her go, Tony," Jayden took a step into the kitchen.

"Don't come any further." Tony jabbed Chloe with the gun. He pulled her to the side so he could see Dave and Jayden both. Dave was just inside the doorway.

Jayden met Chloe's eyes. She gave a tiny wink in his direction. "I'm not feeling well, Tony. I need to sit down, please."

"Stop. I'm not letting you away from me." He tightened his grip around her waist.

Chloe kept her eyes on Jayden, mouthed the words "I love you" and let her knees buckle. She closed her eyes on the way down. Her fall caught Tony off guard and he loosened his grip. A shot rang out and Tony fell backwards. The gun flew out of his hand. Dave was at his side in an instant, kicking the gun out of the way.

"Bastard." Tony sneered at Jayden as he held his shoulder where the bullet had gone clean through.

"It's a flesh wound. You'll live." Jayden rushed to Chloe.

She opened her eyes and smiled as he pulled her close. "I didn't really faint."

"I know. I love you. Don't ever do that again to me."

"I love you, Jayden. I just want all this over and behind us so we can start fresh." She hugged him close. She could feel his heart beating with the adrenal that was pumping through him. "You did it. You saved me."

EPILOGUE

Chloe was wrapped in an afghan curled up on Carla's couch. Jayden had taken Tony to the hospital before going to the station. Dave had given her a ride. He was just as anxious to see Jocelyn as Chloe had been to see Jayden.

She held the cup of peppermint tea that Carla had prepared and enjoyed the warmth. Jocelyn and Dave were talking quietly in the corner while Carla dropped on the couch next to Chloe.

"Are you feeling okay? I think you should be checked by the doctor," Carla spoke softly.

Chloe gripped Carla's hand. "I'm fine. I'll call the doctor tomorrow, but right now I just want to be here with friends, and wait for Jayden."

"Did you finally end up telling him about the baby?"

Chloe smiled. "Yeah. He didn't head for the hills." Chloe shifted to face Carla. "I really do love him."

Carla hugged her close. "Thank God you two came to your senses. Jocelyn and I were afraid we were going to have to lock you in a room together so you would get the hint."

Chloe laughed. "We should consider that for Joce and David. Though maybe those two are finally coming around too."

"Talking about us?" Jocelyn came over and sat on the floor in front of Chloe.

"Just wondering how long you two were going to waste time."

David sank into the recliner. "Really? You want to talk about us? Do you realize the amount of turmoil you brought into Jayden's life?" He shook his head.

Jocelyn winked at Chloe. "Well, maybe I'll be getting a sister out of this whole fiasco."

"Don't rush things." Chloe looked shocked, but her eyes sparkled with her love for Jayden. "I'm not sure after all this your brother won't want some peace and quiet."

"Peace and quiet sounds good." Jayden's voice announced his entrance. Chloe met his eyes and her heart swelled. "Are you going to join me for that R&R?"

He walked slowly across the room and bent to capture her lips. His tongue caressing hers gently, but with her soft moan the kiss became more demanding. As he broke away, he whispered, "I take that as a yes."

"Yes." Chloe nodded.

Jayden glanced around at the others. "Do you mind if I steal her away for just a moment?"

There were murmurs of encouragement. He laced his fingers with hers and led her out to the back flower garden. Standing next to a red rose bush, he pulled her close. "I don't ever want to go through that again. I thought I'd lost you."

Chloe held his face between her hands. "Never. I'm here. I had every confidence that you would be there for me."

"I want to be there for you, Chloe, forever. All this has just made me realize how deep my love goes for you. I want to spend the rest of our days together, raise this baby, and others, if you are willing."

She searched his face and saw the same love shining from his eyes that she felt in her heart. "Are you...?"

"Marry me, Chloe. I don't want to waste another minute without you by my side."

"Yes, God, yes." Chloe slid her arms around his neck and pulled him close, kissing him to seal the deal.

CONTACT

emmaleighreed.com

Facebook – facebook.com/pages/
Emma-Leigh-Reed-Author/392232914212183

Twitter – twitter.com/emmaleighreed

Made in the USA
Columbia, SC
31 October 2020